# DRIFTER

*The Cord Chantry Saga*

## LEE EVERETT

# CHAPTER ONE

**Wyoming Territory**
**August 1868**

The sweltering heat was almost too much for the weary travelers to endure. Dust cascading outside the dilapidated stagecoach station worked well to obscure the view off into the distance as miniature dust devils carried the waves of sand to and fro. Occasionally, the dust would throw itself inside the door of the shack to annoy those waiting inside who were trying to remain out of its clutches, but were having considerable trouble doing so.

Morning sun glazed the landscape, slowly baking it and deterring any type of creature from wanting to venture outside unless absolutely necessary. The land was void of any movement except for that of several buzzards who were circling overhead patiently waiting for something, or even someone, to concede to the parched landscape and provide them with their next meal. Off in the distance, the waves of intense heat could be seen dancing across the horizon, relentlessly teasing and challenging anyone to try to reach them.

Inside the stagecoach station, the meager shelter offered little relief from the intense heat. Those waiting for the incoming stage were at the mercy of the elements as they waited to be rescued from this place and carried somewhere where the range of conditions were much more suitable and abundant.

Madeline Stafford dabbed at her forehead relentlessly with the back of her hand, trying anything she could think of to overcome the heat. She had been the last of the group to arrive, yet she was clearly the one overcome the most by the temperature. Dressed in a blue gingham and calico floor-length skirt and cream long-sleeve blouse she watched those around her, eyeing each of them with interest, especially the man sitting in the far corner with his back against the wall.

She was from the east, a woman in her early twenties who had already experienced far more than any woman her age should have been subjected to. Having lost both her father and mother, her only remaining family besides her brother, to a fire, she had left everything she had known to separate herself from the darkness that had enveloped her life. She had been close to her parents, closer than most children and was hit hard by their passing. She doubted she would ever get over the loss and chose to start her life elsewhere, removing herself from anything and anyone that reminded her of them, her desire to escape having led her here to be with her only sibling.

Though she tried to remain poised and confident, the man's interest caused an uneasiness to creep over her. She had stolen glances at the man throughout the entire time they had been waiting together and noticed that he had not engaged anyone in conversation nor had he made any sort of gesture to invite anyone else to approach him. She dared not try to do so herself and feared that he would approach her, knowing that there would be no one to help her and very little she could do to dissuade his advances if he did.

Twice she had caught him staring at her, probably not intentionally she told herself and more from boredom, but still enough to make her feel uncomfortable, nonetheless. Had there been anywhere else she could have positioned herself to remove herself from his sight she would have gladly done so but the sparse, cramped quarters was nothing more than a few small tables and adjoining chairs and left little room to move about freely. At least for the time being, she was a prisoner to the station.

Quickly losing the last hint of the remaining patience she had managed to salvage, she stood and impatiently walked over to the window of the station to look outside, hoping that her doing so would somehow hurry the stagecoach's arrival. She could sense the stranger's look upon her back now even more than before, but at this point, it didn't matter. Her main concern now was to get to Benton Springs as soon as possible with as little interaction with anyone as necessary, especially the quiet stranger.

Outside, standing under the scant overhang of the station was a young man who looked to be no more than twenty years of age, too young to be a drifter while still too old to require the accompaniment of someone older. She watched through the window as he paced about, periodically stealing glances down the dusty road and impatiently moving about as if ants had invaded his trousers. With nothing in sight to view and no one really to talk to she could tell his immature nature was showing boldly and he was anxious to move on to somewhere else where there were more people and more appealing surroundings to take in.

The young man was sporting a gun belt, much like others his own age in this part of the territory did, though she doubted he had enough experience with the weapon to justify wearing it. Taking into account how young and inexperienced he probably was she surmised that it was probably something he wore more for show in order to fit in than to solicit challenges. She feared if anyone did happen to test his level of skill with it he would no doubt come out on the losing end of things.

After being further annoyed by the stagecoach's delay she returned to her seat as she looked over the only other passengers who were also in wait. A middle-aged man wearing a dark wool suit and a matching bowler hat caught her eye, returning the faint smile she had mustered up on his behalf. She reasoned that he must have traveled a great deal, perhaps some sort of a salesman judging from the large, well weathered suitcase sitting by his side that had obviously been dragged around to quite a few places as if he had been living out of it for quite some time. Her fear was that he would try to solicit her business in whatever he were peddling.

There was also another man, perhaps a few years older than her own age of twenty-three, whom she could tell even when he was sitting down that he was taller than most, wearing a dark, tailored pinstriped suit and matching Stetson. It was obviously that the suit was of an expensive nature right down to the crisp starched white shirt and red Duncan satin Buff tie. The man smiled at her, tipping his hat out of respect before casually returning to lazily shuffling the deck of cards he had been handling so skillfully.

Her glance once again returned to the stranger in the corner, more out of curiosity than anything else. He had not given her a reason to dislike him, but regardless, she felt somewhat distressed by his attention. She hated herself for putting a negative label on the man without having talked to him or even knowing anything about him, but still there was something about him that she found unappealing, but still non-threatening. Having been on her own as of late, she preferred to distance herself from strangers, especially those she felt uncomfortable around.

His quiet demeanor gave her pause and did not bode well with her concerning the upcoming ride. It would be bad enough that she would have to share a coach ride with him, much less be forced to possibly engage him in polite conversation at some point. She did not look forward to such an awkward encounter with him in such a confined space staring across their seats from one another for the remainder of her trip. She knew at some point it would inevitably become necessary for them to speak. In an attempt to avoid such an uncomfortable situation she had already committed herself to looking out the window as much as possible to avoid his glare.

Her thoughts were interrupted as the distant sound of an incoming stage brought her out of her dilemma. With the sound of hooves and creaking wagon wheels descending upon them, she stood relieved and walked over to the window to see it finally rolling into the station. She heard the driver calling out the horses as it came to a stop, the trailing dust it had churned up drifting past it and off into the distance ahead of it. So preoccupied was she of leaving that she had started out the door when she suddenly remembered her bag sitting on the floor next to her chair. By the time she had walked back and picked it up the middle-aged man in the dark suit and bowler had already anxiously claimed her spot at the door. When she joined him just inside of it, he politely tipped his hat to her.

"Begging your pardon, miss," he stated apologetically. "I didn't mean to take your place."

She looked at him closer, a man of obvious means, well mannered and well-kept and freshly smelling of something akin to soap weed. "It's quite alright, sir," she lied as she smiled while trying to remain polite. "I was in no hurry to board. I doubt it will leave without me."

They both watched as the driver of the stage set the brake and climbed down, leaving the foreman sitting in his seat next to him. Judging from his awareness of the surroundings and the fact that he was brandishing a messenger shotgun across his lap, his feet were most assuredly resting on one or more payroll bags of some kind that were conveniently tucked out of sight.

She watched his cautious eye as everyone filed out of the station, his stern look and the serious nature of his job not lost on those wishing to board. His face was tanned from too many days atop a stage and his eyes almost glinted shut from the brightness of the morning. Though so much exposure had left him with nothing more than tiny slits from which to see through his demeanor was such that there was no disputing that he was acutely aware of everything going on around him and was ready to react accordingly.

"Ten minutes, folks," the driver announced aloud as he passed them on his way around the side of the station to relieve himself. "We leave in ten minutes."

After graciously allowing her to move past him, Madeline Stafford took the lead from the man in the suit and was reaching for the door of the stagecoach when a hand reached past her and opened it before she could do so. She noticed that the sleeve wasn't that of the man with the bowler and turned to see that it belonged to the stranger.

She briefly looked into his eyes, so light in color that they were almost grey, becoming startled and unable to respond immediately, but was finally able to summon enough composure to force a faint smile. "Thank you," she finally uttered out of politeness as she grabbed her skirt and pulled it up just high enough to allow her to step inside. As she entered the stagecoach, she was startled by the colored man with a shaved head who was already inside and had apparently come in from a previous destination.

His presence surprised her, catching her off-guard and rendering her absent of a greeting until he decided to speak first. "Morning', ma'am", he gestured politely with a soft nod for lack of a hat. She tried to hide her fluster with her own nod and another faint smile.

"Good morning," she responded as she settled herself into her seat. She watched as the stranger held the door for the other passengers to climb inside, first the man with the bowler, then the well-dressed man with the cards and finally the impatient young man. As they all took their seats she was preoccupied watching the stranger outside the window and felt the stage tilt slightly to the left from his weight as he climbed up onto the boot while holding his gear and rifle. She could hear him tucking his saddlebags onto the rack on the roof before jumping down and climbing through the door to take a seat next to the young man and the colored man. His eyes met hers as he tucked his long legs as close to the bottom of the cramped seat as possible.

"Looks like we're in for another scorcher," the man with the bowler announced to no one in particular as he looked around for someone to take his lead and engage him in conversation. He waited until she glanced his direction and took the gesture as interest. "Don't remember it being this hot this early in the day since I was in Prescott, Arizona after the gold rush. Now that was a hot place." He smiled broadly and extended his hand to her. "Names Sanders. Holbrook Sanders."

"Pleased to meet you, Mr. Sanders. Madeline Stafford," she responded with another smile as they shook hands while reaching around the gambler.

"What brings you out here in this desolate part of the

country, Miss Stafford?" he asked, sporting a well-rehearsed smile.

"I'm on my way to see my brother and his wife in Benton Springs. They recently wed and have a baby on the way. I'm going out there to help them settle into their new home and prepare for its arrival."

"Ah, how lovely. Nothing like seeing a new baby come into the world," Holbrook Sanders announced as he looked away in a melancholy glance. "I've got two sons back home in Texas. Don't get to see them as often as I would like since I travel so much."

"What line of work are you in, Mr. Sanders?" she inquired.

"I work for the railroad, ma'am. I scout new routes that can be built for train tracks. It's a busy job. That's why I carry this satchel with me everywhere I go," he announced as he patted his hand on the oversized satchel resting in his lap. "Has my whole job in it. Maps, plans, land surveys, geological studies, everything you need to build a railroad. Takes me all across the frontier. Y'know, train travel is the future. Yep, we're gonna put these stagecoaches out of business before too much longer. They were fine in their heyday, but I'm afraid they've outlived their usefulness. Pretty soon, no one will want to stay packed into these cramped quarters when they can ride in comfort with all the space they need and with no dust and a lot smoother ride. Why, you can even take in a meal on them."

The comment caused the colored man sitting across for him to scoff softly under his breath, not intentionally to disrupt the conversation, but still loud enough for Holbrook Sanders to pick up on it. "What's the matter, friend?" he asked politely. "Do you not agree that the train will take over the stagecoach industry?"

The colored man nodded gently. "Yeah, I believe it will, but it's going to take awhile before that happens."

"Why do you say that, mister..."

"Nathan Brooks," the colored man stated as they shook hands. "Because I've spent the last seven years building those tracks all over the territory and I'm here to tell you it ain't an easy job. Takes a lot of time. You only average maybe five or six miles of track a day, and that's if it's level."

While Nathan Brooks and Holbrook Sanders continued their conversation over the inevitable demise of the stagecoach, Madeline Stafford looked Nathan Brooks over. Years of working on a railroad had made him solid and muscular, so much so that he was having difficulty positioning himself in his seat next to the two other men he shared the bench seat with. The only saving grace was the smaller stature of the young man sitting next to him between he and the stranger.

She diverted her eyes at him when she was sure he wasn't looking. Although not quite as broad shouldered as Nathan Brooks, the stranger was still a menacing figure by his own right. At six-feet-two, he moved about with the ease of a man much smaller. His rigid jaw was square and firmly set, making him ruggedly handsome and the brim of his hat covered his face, except for the piercing grey eyes that peered from beneath. She considered his looks to be overshadowed by his quietness, but she knew they would still be noticeable to any woman he came into contact with.

As Brooks and Sanders continued sharing notes on the railroad, the driver emerged from behind the station and checked to ensure the door was latched shut as he looked through the window inside the coach. "Okay folks. We're headin' out."

# CHAPTER TWO

A stout call from the driver sent the stagecoach into motion as it lurched forward before finally settling into a faster rhythm. The team of six black Shires pulled the wagon with ease, their immense power showing through in their movements as dust kicked up from their massive hooves drifted into the stage compartment. Doing so quickly forced the group to pull down the shades sparsely covering the windows in an attempt to discourage its invasion. The saving grace was that the breeze created by the fast moving stage was welcoming to all as a way of trying to beat back the heat.

As they continued settling in for the ride, Holbrook Sanders watched the man in the tailored suit sitting next to him quietly handling his deck of cards as if it were an extension of his own hands. His skill was evident from the countless hours he had obviously spent mastering his craft. Sanders took it as another opportunity to strike up a conversation with a fellow traveler. "Might I take it from your fascination with those cards that you are a gambler by trade?"

"I am not certain if I would actually call it a trade, sir, but yes, I am a gambler," he responded, his strong creole accent bleeding through as he extended his hand and continued with a slight, slow nod and a confident smile. "River Holloway, at your service."

"Pleased to meet you, mister Holloway," Sanders exclaimed as they shook. "Holbrook Sanders," he repeated in the event that Holloway had not heard his previous introduction. "River is an interesting name. Might I inquire is there a clever reference behind such a noteworthy appellation?"

"Indeed there is, sir. You see, I was born on the banks of the Mississippi," Holloway said as he continued shifting his cards from hand to hand without looking. "My mother loved the river so and, as a result, decided to forever instill it's presence onto me with such an auspicious title. And please, call me 'River'."

"Well River, what brings you so far from the Mississippi?" Holbrook Sanders inquired as he sat engulfed in the stranger's story.

"I needed a change of scenery, Mr. Sanders. I'm sorry to say the great Mississippi River is no longer the genteel atmosphere that I remember it being during my upbringing. I'm afraid it is now overloaded with gamblers and card sharks who's sole purpose is to hustle people out of their money. I, myself, do not share in these dealings and felt it was best for me to pursue my interests out west to a new audience where our trade had not been so viciously slandered."

"My names Billy Richmond," the young man chimed in with a broad smile without warning as he panned the faces of the group for someone to talk to.

"And what brings you out west, young William?" Holbrook Sanders asked as he took the bait to redirect his attention over to him.

"My uncle has a ranch just outside of Benton Springs. He wired my folks so time ago and told them I could come work it, if I wanted. But then they passed and he was left as my only relative. Said if things went well he would carve me off a small piece of his land for myself and I could work it and make it my own place. Of course, that would take some time, but at least he offered."

"That sounds delightful, William," Holbrook Sanders exclaimed. "You are truly a lucky young man to have such generous elders who are willing to share their prosperity with you. Good for you." The comment brought an even bigger smile to Billy's face as he sat back in his seat beaming with pride at his opportunity.

Madeline Stafford had sat quietly listening to everyone share their intentions while anxiously waiting for the stranger to join in the discussions, but as of yet he had not seemed interested in doing so. She had exchanged glances with the man, who had yet to utter even a single word, until she could no longer contain her curiosity. "I noticed we have not heard from you, sir," she started as she looked into his eyes. "Would you be so kind as to tell us your name, if I might ask?"

"Cord Chantry," the stranger reluctantly answered as he tipped the brim of his hat to her.

"And what is the nature of *your* trip, Mr. Chantry?" she asked with interest.

"The usual. What drifters do."

"Come now, Mr. Chantry," she beseeched, "you must give us more than that."

"I'm afraid I'm rather dull."

"Now, you must let us decide that for ourselves."

Cord wanted to end the discussion but he could see the young lady wasn't going to allow him to do so. He reluctantly continued. "I'm also heading to work a ranch," Cord Chantry stated flatly. "It belongs to a good friend of mine whose is expanding. He needed the help and I needed work so the match made sense."

She was intrigued by his answer. "If you are a ranch hand,

then where is your horse?" she inquired, testing his response. "I imagine it will be difficult to perform such work without one."

"It died," Cord Chantry informed her calmly with a placated glance. "Stomped into a pit of rattlesnakes."

"Oh, I'm so sorry to hear that, Mr. Chantry," she retreated from her questioning. "I wasn't aware that it had fallen victim to such a horrific outcome. My apologies for my candid questioning."

"You weren't even able to keep the saddle?" Holbrook Sanders asked curiously.

"Tried carrying it for awhile," Chantry said in response followed by a faint smile, "but it got too darn heavy, especially in this heat. Finally had to leave it out on the plains."

"How unfortunate," Sanders stated. "I hope there was no sentimental attachment to it."

"Nothing sentimental, but I still hated to leave it behind. I do miss the horse more than the saddle."

"What type of horse was it?" she asked, unsure of why it mattered.

"Paint," Cord Chantry answered. "Spent three years with that horse. Best one I ever owned."

"There was nothing that could be done for the beast?" Holbrook Sanders asked.

"A horse has a chance at surviving a snake bite, but not when there's three of 'em."

The conversation lagged over the next half-hour as they continued down the bumpy trail, jostled about by the uneven terrain that passed as the road. The rhythmic swaying of the stage was irritating to Cord Chantry, who always preferred being on the back of a horse instead of being sealed inside of a stagecoach, which was cramped and more or less void of fresh air. He had never enjoyed the confines of a stage and had always gone out of his way to avoid using them. *He couldn't wait to be rid of the carriage so he could enjoy fresh air again.*

The landscape was mostly barren except for being dotted with pinyon trees and scrub brush with an occasional tumbleweed passing by them off in the distance. Off to their left was a jagged mountain range, the hillsides generously painted with greenery giving it the allure of a cooler, more appealing scenery.

The dry season had already hit hard this year as evident to the almost continuous sheet of sand blowing about, making the already sweltering heat that much more uncomfortable and irritating to endure. On one occasion a jackrabbit was poised on it's hind legs as it watched the stage pass by before darting off out of sight to safety within the brush. Having virtually exhausted all avenues of small talk, everyone had abandoned their questioning of one another, expect for an occasional stray comment here and there and had settled into their ride. Young Billy Richmond had even managed to doze off with his head hanging forward onto his chest when the shot rang out.

Cord Chantry tensed up, instantly knowing what was happening. He reached into his boot and removed a small revolver he kept stayed there, tucking it into the back of his waistband without comment. Madeline Stafford also heard the shot, but had not put the meaning behind it together with the sound until she saw Chantry remove the trigger guard from his gun belt. He lifted the window flap and was staring intently out the window when they heard the driver calling out to the team to stop as the stagecoach quickly lurched to a halt.

"What's happening?" she asked, a look of concern forming on her face as she glanced from one side of the stagecoach to another, but Cord Chantry was too enthralled in what was going on outside to answer her. It was then that they heard the horses coming up to the stagecoach. Madeline watched silently as Cord drew his gun in anticipation, his gaze glaring outside as it remained fixed on the men who had ridden up.

"You inside the stage, come out with you hands up!" they heard a man yell. "And don't try anything or the driver dies!"

Madeline was visibly shaken by the threat. "What do we do?" she asked Cord Chantry.

"We do as he says," Chantry answered as he reluctantly holstered his weapon. He held up his right hand as he slowly opened the stage door with his left one and stepped out. He took a few steps over to allow room for the other passengers to disembark, all the while closely watching the four men lined up before him on horseback all of whom had their guns covering them. As the rest of the group exited the stage, Chantry glanced up at the foreman who was slumped over the side railing dead, his shotgun having fallen onto the floor next to his feet as the driver sat quietly with his hands up. One of the men, who looked to be around Chantry's age, spoke next.

"Everybody do as they're told and no one else gets hurt," the man stated firmly as he turned to one of the other riders. "You," the man said motioning to Cord Chantry. "Drop your gun."

Chantry carefully slipped the gun from his holster and dropped it onto the ground in front of him. "Now, you" the man motioned to Billy Richmond. He watched as Billy disposed of his gun in like fashion and glanced at the other passengers to see if any of them were carrying a weapon before he was satisfied.

"Earl, grab those payroll bags," he said as one of the men jumped down from his horse and climbed up the side of the stage. The man chuckled as he threw four bags down onto the ground before jumping down himself.

"Plen, get their wallets," the same man ordered as the first man started gathering the bags. A jovial man laughed indiscreetly as he hopped down from his horse and quickly retrieved a burlap sack from his saddlebag. He giggled to himself as he hurried over to the first of the group, delighted that he had been chosen to take such an important part of the holdup.

He started with the gambler, River Holloway, as he held the sack out in front of him and waited for him to empty his pockets into it. When he had fished his belongings from his pockets, the robber appeared unconvinced that he had given them everything and took it upon himself to stuff his hands into Holloway's pockets to see for himself. When he came across a pocket watch he pulled it from his pocket and threw it into the bag before giving Holloway an irritated look while Holloway stared at the man without a reaction.

Next, he stepped over to Holbrook Sanders and then Madeline Stafford, a sly tobacco-stained smile spreading over his face as he stared at her. She placed her necklace that she had removed into the bag and waited, but the man did not move on to the next person. The man who had ordered the collection of belongings that Chantry perceived as being the apparent leader of the group, was starting to grow impatient.

"What are you waiting for, Plen? Get their stuff and let's go."

"I think she's got something else, Virgil," the man called Plen announced with a devilish grin. "I think there's something hiding under that there dress of hers."

Madeline looked at Plen, her face clearly showing that she was becoming more and more uncomfortable with every passing second. "Forget it," the leader, Virgil, spoke up in a harsh tone. "Just get what you can find and let's get out of here. We aren't even supposed to be out here."

Plen paused at the order, unwilling to give up on searching her so easily until his hesitation angered the leader, Virgil.

"Damn it, Plen, I said let's go!" Virgil yelled.

Plen's nefarious grin dissipated as he reluctantly moved on to Nathan Brooks. Plen's reaction to the sight of the colored man was one of surprise as if it were the first time that he had noticed his darker skin.

"Look at this one, Virgil," Plen announced with a mischievous grin. "Don't see many colored folk in these parts." His self-imposed giggling faded away as he caught sight of the small medallion on a gold necklace hanging around Nathan's neck. Plen's eyes widened at the sight of it and he immediately knew he wanted it for his own.

"What are you waiting for?!" Virgil argued as Plen had already started reaching for Nathan's necklace, but stopped when Nathan grabbed the man's wrist firmly with his hand.

"You ain't getting my necklace," Nathan declared, his face hard and stoic. "You can take my money and everything else I own, but there ain't no way this necklace is coming off from around my neck. My mama gave me this necklace right before she died and it stays with me."

The defiance did not sit well with Plen as his smile quickly faded to a more serious expression. He was so caught by surprise by the man's resistance that he didn't know how to respond, his face twisted in anger as he jerked his hand free of Nathan's grasp. When he reached for the necklace again, Nathan made his move.

He grabbed Plen by the front of his shirt with both hands and quickly pulled him towards him, head butting him in the nose, shattering it. Plen squealed out in agony as he dropped to his knees. The distraction was just what Cord Chantry had been waiting for.

With the robbers assuming Chantry was unarmed and with his hands hanging down by his side he reached around and quickly drew the spare gun from his waistband, firing first at the leader Virgil and then at the man next to him, hitting both before they knew to fire themselves. He was about to turn his weapon on the third man standing next to his horse when he heard a shot being fired from Billy Richmond's gun that he had picked up from the ground during the commotion, striking the third man who had been preoccupied with tying the payroll bags onto his horse. The shot sent him to the ground where his friends had already fallen. The entire exchange lasted only a few seconds, but when it was over three men lay dead and the fourth was lying on the ground rolling about back and forth applying pressure to his broken nose, his muffled screaming under his breath heard through his fingers wrapped across his face.

Plen didn't resist as Nathan Brooks grabbed the man's gun from his holster and tossed it off to the side out of his reach. Plen was too preoccupied with his pain to respond as he continued rolling around on the ground with blood leaking from under his fingers.

"You broke my nose!" Plen finally yelled at Nathan.

"Try to touch my necklace again and I'll break your neck," Nathan declared as he walked over next to where Cord Chantry had climbed up onto the side of the wagon to check on the foreman before realizing it was too late to help him. Chantry climbed back down and looked over at Nathan. "He's dead." The men focused their attention back on the only surviving member of the holdup gang. By now, Plen had noticed that he was the only one of his companions still alive, all of which now lay dead on the ground. His eyes widened, particularly at the sight of Virgil.

"What have you done?" he asked in an almost panicked tone. "You killed Virgil. Do you know what you've done?"

"We stopped a robbery," Chantry announced without emotion as he picked up his revolver and holstered it.

"His brother is going to kill you, mister!" Plen proclaimed as he continued staring down at the lifeless body. "He's got a gang of twenty men sitting in Benton Springs waiting for us to get there. He owns that town! You'll never get to set foot in it before he shoots every last one of you! When he hears about this, he'll hunt you down and kill you!"

Cord Chantry noticed that it appeared the man's outburst was beginning to trouble Madeline Stafford. "Shut up," Chantry ordered the man. He started to say something else when he saw a rider appear from behind a small collection of bushes a couple of hundred yards or so ahead of them on the road and stare at the group quickly before spurring his horse into motion towards town. Chantry watched the man quickly disappear behind the dust his horse kicked up. "Who was that?"

Plen ignored the question as he continued sitting up on his knee nursing his nose. Chantry walked over to the man and grabbed the front of the his blood-soaked shirt, yanking him to his feet in one swift motion. "Who was that?" he repeated in a harsher tone while staring into Plen's eyes.

"That's our insurance in case anything went wrong," Plen announced smugly. "He's on his way back to town to tell Frank Quincey. When he gets here he'll see that you killed his baby brother in cold blood. You're a dead man."

# CHAPTER THREE

Cord Chantry looked at the cloud of dust getting smaller off in the distance as the rider quickly ventured out of his sight. "Why didn't we go after him?" Billy Richmond walked up and asked as he looked in the direction that Chantry was looking.

"We would have never caught him," Chantry admitted. "He had too much of a head start on us."

The young man questioned the validity of the reason. "How do you know that for sure?" he asked.

"Yeah, how can you be sure?" Holbrook Sanders added.

Chantry answered them as he turned back to the stage. "Because the horses are gone."

Everyone's attention was suddenly diverted to looking around the stage. It was the first time they had noticed that during all of the commotion none of them had realized that the robber's horses had run away during the shootout. As everyone glanced around them in all directions it became evident to them that they were nowhere in sight nor did anyone even know which direction they had gone.

"What'll we do now?" River Holloway asked as he dug his

possessions out of the burlap sack and began systematically replacing them in their designated pockets.

"We can't stay here, that's for sure. We need to get over to Hurley," Chantry answered. "And the only way to do that is to find those horses."

"Why Hurley?" Nathan inquired while walking over to Chantry. "Why not just keep going straight to Benton Springs?"

"Because what he said is true," Chantry answered as he nodded his head towards Plen, who threw him a disgusted glare in return.

"How do you know that?" Holbrook Sanders argued. "You're just going to take the word of a thief and a killer? How do we know he's even telling the truth? He probably just said that to throw us off."

"No, he's telling the truth," Chantry answered. "I've heard for awhile now that Frank Quincey had taken over Benton Springs, but till now I thought it was just a rumor. Guess it wasn't."

"And you're gonna believe the word of that idiot?" River Holloway questioned as he pointed to a defeated Plen.

Chantry turned to face the two men. "I don't have to. Frank Quincey is known for always riding with a large group of men. If we try to stroll into town they'll cut us down before we reach the first building. There's no cover leading into town, not from any direction. The town is built in the middle of a flat prairie. We'd be sitting ducks."

"What about the law?" River asked.

"Quincey controls the law. They don't take a step without Frank Quincey telling them where to plant their boot."

"Why aren't we going back to Jackson Creek?" Holbrook Sanders inquired.

"Because Jackson Creek is a very small community with hardly anyone there. There would be nowhere to hide and no one to protect us. Frank Quincey and his men would take over the town and burn it to the ground in a heartbeat to get us out in the open. We wouldn't stand a chance. Hurley is big enough to protect us with a good sheriff backing it. It's our only shot."

Madeline scoffed loud enough for everyone to hear her. "So, we're just gonna run with our tails between…"

Her comment was cut short by a gunshot from behind them. Cord Chantry whirled around while simultaneously drawing his gun only to see the stagecoach driver drop the foreman's shotgun while clutching his chest as a result of a shot from Plen. Chantry fired, hitting Plen and dropping him face down onto the ground. He cursed under his breath at lowering his guard enough for the man to get a shot off at the driver.

Chantry and Nathan Brooks ran over and caught the driver just before he fell over the side of the front seat. They gingerly handled the man, lowering him onto the ground and then checking his wound to the chest. The man was struggling to gain a breath as a trickle of blood began running out of the side of his mouth. He began mouthing words that were laced with bloody drool. Chantry and Nathan knew there was nothing that could be done for the man out here.

"Payrolls," he whispered as he coughed up more blood while staring at them.

"Payrolls?" Chantry asked softly. "What about the payrolls?"

"Miner's and railroad payrolls," the dying man said between coughs. "They were on the stage."

Chantry glanced over to Nathan. One of the men they had killed had tied the bags to his horse. Now, that horse had run off carrying all that money on its back.

"Take it with you," the man sputtered, his speech

drowning in blood, his breathing becoming raspy. "Get it to the sheriff in Hurley. Looks like I have to trust you, mister."

"How much is in there?" Nathan asked the man.

"Twenty-seven thousand," the man proclaimed as his head slowly tilted to the side and his breathing stopped with one final exhale. Chantry heard Madeline gasp at the sight as he slowly stood and stared down at the man and then at everyone as they gathered around him, his face blanketed in urgency. "We've got to get our hands on those horses."

"Yeah. We can't leave that kind of money behind for those thieves," River Holloway exclaimed.

Chantry looked over at the man. "I'm not worried as much about the money as I am getting our hands on those horses and getting out of here before Frank Quincey and his gang show up."

"How are we going to find the horses?" Nathan asked. "We don't even know which way they headed."

Cord Chantry pulled his revolver and dumped the empty cartridges, replacing them with fresh ones as he explained. "Each of you take a gun belt and head in a different direction. As soon as someone sees the horses, fire a single shot. That'll signal to whoever is closer to come help while the rest of us meet back here. Just don't go too far out or you might get lost. Then we'll have a whole new problem to deal with. And make sure you hurry. They'll be on their way here before you know it." He then turned to Madeline. "You stay here."

The comment did not sit well with the woman. "Why do I need to do that? Is it because I'm a woman because I can help, too. I can..."

"It has nothing to do with that," he interrupted, irritated that he had to correct her. "It would be better if you and Mr. Sanders stayed here with the stage and our things until the horses are brought back. We don't need you getting lost out there. Take the time to go through your belongings to take out what you'll need. Leave everything else behind that you can. The lighter we can travel, the better off we'll be."

"Fine by me," Sanders graciously agreed as he walked over and took a seat in the doorway of the stagecoach. Madeline didn't respond to the idea, but instead, remained quiet. Chantry could tell from her expression that she was offended, but she would have to save her bitterness for a later argument since he didn't have time to argue the point.

Everyone dispersed and began removing the gun belts from the dead robbers. Chantry was walking past Nathan Brooks and saw the man pull the gun from a gun belt. "Do you know how to use..." he had almost finished asking the question when he saw Nathan pull the hammer back and roll the cylinder down his arm smoothly to check the chambers before releasing the hammer in one swift motion, spin the gun and tuck it neatly into the holster. Chantry was impressed. "Well, never mind," he added as Nathan looked at him as he slung the gun belt over his shoulder.

Once everyone had a weapon, including Madeline, Chantry assigned each of the men a direction and they all headed out, leaving Holbrook Sanders and a fuming Madeline standing in the shade of the stagecoach, hurt and insulted at the same time.

Frank Quincey and two of his men were sitting in the Palomino Saloon in Benton Springs when the batwing doors flew open and one of his riders came rushing in with a despondent look on his face, frantically looking for the man. Once he had spotted Quincey, he moved straight towards his table. When he had filtered his way through the crowd and made it over to him he was slightly out of breath and sweating profusely from a combination of the stress of the news he was being forced to deliver and the hurried ride into town.

Frank Quincey looked up from his discussion with his men, still sporting a huge smile as the laughter they were enjoying slowly started to dissipate around him and everyone, including those in the saloon that were not even part of his group, stopped all of their activities to hear the news that the frantic man had come to deliver. By the time the man had made it over to Quincy's table, the silence inside the saloon was deafening.

"Frank," the man uttered in urgency as he struggled to take in a breath, "Virgil's been shot."

Frank sat his glass down as he slowly stood and faced the man with a deadpan expression without ever losing eye contact. "What do you mean he's been shot?"

"Virgil and some of us robbed the Silver Line Stage outside of town...," the man began explaining, but before he could finish, Frank Quincey took a menacing step towards him. The man reacted by taking a small step back, fearing the wrath that Quincey was about to unleash onto him.

"What do you mean you robbed it?" Frank Quincey uttered, looking at him through hard, level eyes, his voice filled with anger. "Who told you to do that?"

The man took another small step back, holding his hands up as a defense. "It was all Virgil's idea, Frank," the man said in a desperate plea, his voice starting to crack. "He thought it would be a good idea. He wanted to do something on his own. He planned the whole thing right down to the last detail."

"Except for the detail of getting shot," Frank uttered angrily. He looked back at the man as he realized he had been too distracted by the news to ask the other obvious important question. "Is Virgil okay?"

The man's face was blank and despondent as he feared

what Quincey would do to him when he gave him the answer he knew he wasn't going to like to hear. "I don't know," he responded in a sheepish tone. "Maybe. I don't know. I was too far away to get a good look."

"What do you mean you were too far away?" Frank demanded to know. "Where were you?"

"Virgil had me stay back a couple hundred yards and watch what happened. He wanted me to be out of range in case things got out of hand and then I could make it back here to tell you."

"If you were that far away then how do you know he got shot? Did you actually see it?"

"I heard shooting, but I don't know where it came from and I saw Virgil and the others fall off their horses."

Frank Quincey carefully mulled over the details that he was hearing. "But you aren't sure if they're okay or if they're dead?"

"No," the man had started to calm down a little since seeing Quincy's reaction soften. "Like I said I was too far away."

A despondent Frank Quincey halted his advancements and looked away as he pondered what the man was telling him. He knew Virgil had always wanted to do a job without his help and had always felt as if he were living in Frank's shadow, but that was now a moot point. Frank knew his brother was still too green and didn't have the thought process to set up and pull off something as complex as a robbery, to make sure that there was a contingency plan in place for every last detail that could possibly arise and to know how to execute that plan in the event that things went south. This was the proof.

Frank Quincey had been committing robberies the better portion of his adult life. He had gotten good at it, to the point that most lawmen in the area dared not even challenge him anymore because of his reputation and his legion of men. He had only been confronted by the outside law twice and it had not boded well for the lawmen on either occasion. He had been reluctant to kill the men out of fear of bringing reprisal on his head from others the likes of which he knew he would not be able to contend with. But two things were certain: those lawmen had left the territory unsuccessful in their attempt and they were fearful to try their hand at bringing him in again. He had thought his problems were finally behind him and now this.

Quincey thought through the scenario. He wasn't at all happy that Virgil had taken it upon himself to rob a stage-coach, especially since he had never been involved in one before. It was an ingenious idea to place a lookout down the road from the actual holdup in the event that something had gone wrong. He had never thought of such a point, but, then again, he had never needed outside help when pulling a job. But this was no time for showering someone with accolades. He needed to know whether or not his brother was still alive. For all he knew, he could be lying out there in the middle of the road hurt, or worse, dying. The rider's vague answers annoyed him even more than Virgil's independence.

"How far out were they?" Quincey asked as he walked over and gathered his hat from off the top of the table.

"Eight to maybe ten miles," the man answered after thinking it over for a few seconds.

"Then we need everybody here."

"Where are they?" the rider asked.

"They're bringing a herd into Calhoun. They should be there now and if they aren't, they'll be there soon. I need you to ride over there and get them. They're to come here as soon as they're finished with the cattle. Understand?"

Quincey grabbed the man's arm as he had turned to lead

Quincey out of the saloon. "Wait a minute. Why didn't any of the people on the stage come after you?"

"They couldn't. The horses ran off right as the shooting started."

"Then that means they'll have to waste some time herding them," Frank Quincey pointed out as he released his grip on the man's arm. "That'll give me time to check on my brother while you go and get the others."

# CHAPTER FOUR

The limbs of the scrub brush slowly parted as Cord Chantry glanced through it while trying not to make a sound. He had been tracking the horses for some time and had almost given up on finding them until luck finally shone on him and he spotted them in the edge of a small grove of trees a little over a mile from the stagecoach. He was both relieved that they had not gone any further than this but, at the same time, he was also concerned about the distance he now had to make up while being desperate to make it back with them.

Out there in the distance in front of him he could see the horses grazing not fifty yards away, some of them curiously raising their heads up into the air as if anticipating his arrival, their snouts pulling in breaths to check for any hint of human in the air. He was able to spot all four of them, a good sign that he would be able to quickly be on the return back to the stage, assuming all of them were willing to let him near them and chose not to flee.

He eased his way from behind the brush, showing his appearance to them early on and standing still long enough for them to become accustomed to his presence. He took great care not to move too suddenly so as not to spook them, hoping they would be accepting of him and realize that he meant them no harm. It was always difficult to know just how a spooked horse would respond to the first person they came into contact with after such a traumatic ordeal so he knew how important it was that he took his time since he might not get another chance. And with Frank Quincey and his men on their way, they didn't have time for a second chance, even if it was available.

As he continued to move closer to the horses, he tried to go through the timeline in his head of how long it had been since they had seen the lookout rider leave heading towards town. He could only guess at how long it had been, but what he did know was that it was long enough to know that they were quickly running out of time.

A lot of what would happen to them would depend on just how quickly Frank Quincey could gather all of his men, but then again, it might not matter once he heard that his brother had been shot. It was possible he would leave with those he had with him at the time and let the rest of them follow along as soon as they were able. Either way, Chantry knew they probably had an hour, maybe less.

There was no way the rider would know how badly Virgil Quincey was injured or whether or not he was even dead, but that level of uncertainty would only manage to spur Frank Quincey on that much more. Chantry had heard of Quincey and knew that he was the type of man that was all consumed with whatever he was involved in. That would include exacting revenge on those that harmed his brother. He would follow them to the ends of the earth to make things right which meant that the only way this was going to end was that he would have to be stopped, a thought that Cord did not look forward to in the least.

He had heard rumors about Frank Quincy's temper, but

he had also heard an equal number of claims concerning his speed with a gun. He was by no means the fastest around, but there had been several instances when he was able to hold his own when a challenge arose.

Dismissing Quincey's threat for the moment, Cord focused on getting the horses back to the group quickly since the rider they had seen leaving had no doubt already reached town by now, or was drawing near, and would be hurriedly gathering Quincey and the rest of his men to return to the stage.

Cord had never met Frank Quincey, but the man's reputation preceded him and Cord had heard enough about him to know that that reputation was bad enough even if it hadn't been embellished through stories. Quincey had a reputation not just as a killer, but a brutal one plain and simple. The man was cold and calculating, just the type of man that was needed to run a gang of outlaws. It was also the very same type that would stop at nothing to get what he wanted, no matter what the cost to human life. He would be willing to lay out his life or that of his men in the name of revenge.

He had seen this type of man more times than he could recall through the years and it had always been the same each and every time. There was no honor to these men, no empathy and no regard for others outside of their group. This type of man took away from others until there was nothing left to take and then they often did away with witnesses more times than not. No one was clear of their wrath for they cared for no one expect family. That was the one true bond that they would be willing to lay their life on the line to protect so Cord knew when Quincey found out that his brother was indeed dead, the man would stop at nothing to exact his revenge. And that revenge would not cease until Cord and the rest of them were all dead.

As he approached the horses, he made slow strides,

making sure to keep his hands showing at all times. He inched his way closer as several of the horses stiffened their ears to take in his movements, as if alerting the others in case they hadn't seen that someone was approaching. As soon as he saw the group stiffen and begin watching him more intently, he paused.

"Easy, boys," he said softly as he once again began carefully moving towards them. One of the horses took a couple of short jumps off to the side, warning Cord that he was considering making a run for it, causing him once again to halt his advancements. *I don't have time for this...*

He crouched down and grabbed a handful of tall grass, offering it to him as a treat and hoping it would take the animal's mind off of his movements long enough for him to start moving closer. He watched the horse's ears flicker and wondered if the beast was actually falling for his deception or if he were simply trying to relay to him that he wasn't being fooled by such an amateur move.

Once he felt the animal had eased back on his anxiousness, he started slowly moving forward again. He made up most of the remainder of the distance between he and the horses without incident, feeling he had finally won over their trust. He was able to get close enough to reach out and take the reins of the closest horse and hold onto him until he could rub the side of his snout while he calmly talked to him. The horse responded by neighing gently as Cord walked around the group grabbing all of their reins. When he had a firm hold on all of them, he climbed into the saddle of one, drew his weapon and fired a single shot above his head. After holstering the weapon, he started the group of horses back to the stagecoach while hoping that he wasn't too late.

A few minutes later when the stage came into view, he could see that River Holloway and Billy Richmond had already returned and were standing next to Madeline. He stopped the animals just short of the group as Billy walked over and helped him tie the horses securely to the back of the stage. The two then joined River and Madeline in the shade of the stage. Cord noticed that Madeline had changed out of her long skirt and shoes and into a pair of tan jeans and riding boots.

"Any sign of riders?" Cord asked as they walked up to the two, choosing not to bring attention to her change of wardrobe.

"No, nothing," Madeline answered. "Thank goodness you found the horses."

"Yeah, they were just over that hill, grazing," Cord responded as he glanced around the area. "Any sign of Nathan?"

"No, haven't seen him," Madeline said. "Hopefully, he wasn't too far away to hear the shot."

"I hate to admit it but we might have to leave him," River Holloway chimed in. "We can't wait around here much longer or those men will be here."

"That's true," Holbrook Sanders nodded in agreement. "We have to think of ourselves in a time such as this or none of us will make it."

Cord threw River a disinterested look. "We're not leaving anyone behind. We all leave together or we don't go at all."

"It's just one man," River trying to stress his point. "We cannot put all of us in jeopardy just because of him. It wouldn't be fair to the rest of us. Besides, I am quite sure he would feel the same way about leaving one of us behind."

"We're not leaving," Cord chided in a more aggressive tone as he stared intently at River, who was clearly not amused by the challenge.

"I do not know why that is your call, Mr. Chantry," River responded with contention in his voice as he picked up the gun belt he had been using. "I think we should all have a say in this. We should at least vote on it."

"Not when it comes to leaving someone behind," Cord corrected him as he started checking the saddlebags of the horses. "If you want to leave, go ahead and take a horse, but the rest of us are waiting here for Nathan."

"And what in regards to the money?" River asked, trying not to sound too greedy while changing the subject.

Cord stopped what he was doing and glared over at River with concern. He didn't like the line of questioning from him."What *about* the money?"

"Who shall be in charge of it?" River asked.

"No one's in charge of it. We're all taking it back to town and turning it over to the sheriff to handle."

River desperately wanted to say something, but he did not like the defense that Cord was putting up. He stood quietly and glanced around the group to see what their reactions were. He was more than disappointed to see that no one was backing him up on his decision to leave Nathan behind, not even Holbrook Sanders, whom he had counted on to back him. Frustrated by the lack of support, River scoffed out loud and dropped the gun belt onto the ground, fully disgusted and irritated. He stepped over to the open door of the stage and sat down in the doorway.

Cord looked back at the group. Billy and Madeline silently nodded in agreement while Holbrook Sanders hesitated at first, but after checking to make sure what the others present were deciding he reluctantly joined the decision of the group. He took off his jacket and tossed it into the open window of the stage, tilting his hat back on his head so he could wipe the beads of sweat that had been forming on his forehead from the unrelenting heat.

"Which direction did Nathan go?" Cord asked Madeline as he gathered the reins of the horse he had been handling.

"Over there," she said as she pointed to the east, causing Cord to look off in that direction. "By the way," she added, "I couldn't help but notice that there's six of us and only four horses. Does that mean that some of us going to be riding double?"

Cord's thoughts came back to what she had pointed out. He had been so consumed with getting the horses back that it hadn't occurred to him that there weren't enough of them for everyone. "We'll never make it riding double, not in this heat. It would kill the horses and then we'd really be in a mess. We'll have to take two from the team." He turned to River and Holbrook Sanders. "While Billy starts unhitching them, you two grab whatever we can carry from the stage that you think we'll need while I go after Nathan."

River began climbing up the side of the stage and started tossing items down to Holbrook while Billy went over to the team and began unhooking the two lead horses. Both of the massive animals acted a little uneasy at having their harnesses removed out in the middle of nowhere but he soothed them by talking to them to make sure they were calm. Billy was working on rigging a set of makeshift reins and Cord had just climbed into the saddle and grabbed the reins of one of the robber's horses for Nathan to ride when they heard Madeline call out. "There's Nathan."

Cord looked up to see Nathan come into view from around the front of the stage. By the time he had walked the rest of the distance to them, Cord and Billy had moved the two lead horses over next to the side of the stagecoach.

"I was just about to come looking for you. We're almost ready to go," Cord informed Nathan.

"I'll grab my things," Nathan said as he started digging through his pile of belongings. Cord, Billy, River and Holbrook then began attaching the rest of the supplies onto the horses while Madeline finished going through her bag to remove what she wanted.

"Take only what we need," Cord reminded them. "We don't have room for luxuries. We're going to need to travel fast so make your loads as light as possible."

"It doesn't matter what I bring as long as I bring my satchel," Holbrook Sanders announced to the group.

"We don't have room for your satchel," Cord informed him with a stern tone.

"Mr. Chantry, it doesn't matter if I make it or not as long as this satchel makes it. It contains the entire future of this territory. It simply can not be duplicated, therefore, it must be saved at all costs."

"If you want to keep up with it, then that's on you, but none of the rest of us are responsible for it."

Holbrook nodded in agreement as he pulled the satchel towards him. "Understood. Thank you."

Cord divided up the payroll bags and made sure they were secure to the horses before grabbing his rifle from the items they had removed from the roof of the stage. While everyone else secured the last of their belongings on the backs of the other horses, he went over in his mind which direction they needed to go. In no time, they were all ready to leave.

"I'll take one of the lead horses," Cord decided as he claimed down and walked over, grabbing the reins of one of the stage animals.

"I'll take the other one," Nathan declared.

"Who has the money?" River asked.

"It's split up between me, Nathan and Madeline," Cord informed him. He could tell from River's reaction that the man wasn't okay with the choice, but he was relieved to see that he had refrained from taking the discussion any further since there was no time to debate it. Even so, Cord knew it would not be the last time the man would bring up the subject.

After rendering assistance to Holbrook Sanders, Cord climbed back onto his horse and pulled the reins to face the others. "Everybody ready?" he asked as he scanned the faces of the group. When everyone had nodded to him in agreement he turned his horse towards the west. "Then let's go."

# CHAPTER FIVE

Everyone present in Benton Springs was dumbfounded and shocked by the commotion brought about by the group consisting of Frank Quincey and his men leaving town in a cloud of dust. The group numbered four men in all, including Quincey himself, as they fled the town in a stampede of horses, the thunderous beating of hooves drowning out anything else that was around them.

Frank Quincey's orders to collect his men had been swift and precise. His men had ridden with him long enough to know that their loyalty to him was not up for negotiation. If someone showed that they were unwilling to be completely committed to riding with him, they would be dealt with in the harshest of ways. Quincey had no qualms about removing someone from the group that he felt wasn't living up to his leadership. He only tolerated those hands who happened to be loyal to him. Such unquestionable devotion from these men made the group even more dangerous.

They headed out of town with Quincey not knowing what to expect back at the stage. He only hoped that he made it back to his little brother in time since this was a job that

Virgil had come up without his consent or input. He would have never allowed nor encouraged Virgil to go out on his own just for this very reason, but his brother had always been rather impulsive and impatient and now that impatience could very well have cost him his life.

Over the last few years since Virgil had started riding with him, Frank had tried to protect his little brother as much as possible, which wasn't easy while trying to maintain such a large group of men. The Quincey boys had no family to speak of which caused Virgil to not only look up to Frank as a brother, but also as a mentor. On one occasion, Virgil had tried to give orders to the men, but Frank quickly realize that they did not respect Virgil in the same way as they did him. Now, he wondered how his younger brother had managed to convince some of the men to ride with him on this job.

As of lately, Virgil had gotten it into his head that he wanted to try to do some things on his own. He didn't really care to be in his brother's shadow all the time and wanted to prove to himself, and to his brother, that he could handle things as equally well as his brother Frank. But taking on a job had not been good idea, especially since he had not discussed doing so with Frank. The older Quincey wanted to chastise his little brother for stepping out of bounds, but until he was for certain that the young man was going to be okay, he couldn't think about that at the moment.

The problem lie in the fact that Frank Quincey knew his brother was not ready to take on such a momental task and had tried to dissuade him as much as possible not to do so. The younger Quincey was reckless and impulsive, two traits that caused him to get into several bad predicaments over the years, predicaments that Frank was then forced to pull him out of. Frank felt Virgil's inexperience would be too much of a detriment to him and now, this latest situation had proven Frank right, bringing about his worst fear.

He rode as swiftly as his horse would take him, hoping for the best, but fearing the worst. He only hoped that the rider who had been dispatched from the robbery had not seen things as accurately as he had relayed to him. Judging from the distance the rider had viewed the failed robbery it was likely that he could have been mistaken. At least, that was what Frank was hoping for. What he did know was that if his brother was, heaven forbid, gone, he would take great pleasure in killing everyone that was involved.

The ride to the stage seemed to take forever, the anticipation and the gut-wrenching uncertainty of what he would find there was almost too much for him to endure. Although he dared not let his men see him so distraught, the impatience was there, nonetheless. Finally, after much riding, he saw what he perceived to be the stagecoach coming into view. He pushed his horse on, almost past its limits, placing the compassion he had for his brother over the compassion for the animal he was riding. As they drew closer, he became unsure as to what he saw.

There were four bodies lying on the ground next to the stage, but no sign of any horses and no sign of anyone else. Did that mean the passengers on the stage had taken the horses? The rider had told him the horses had ran away. Did that mean the passengers on the stage were now on foot since the team of horses that had pulled the stage were gone and there was no sign of anyone, just the stagecoach sitting in the middle of the road.

When they pulled up to the scene, Frank began quickly searching the bodies until he saw that one of them was his brother. His heart sank as he looked down at the younger sibling's lifeless body. He dismounted and walked over to him and carefully rolled him over onto his back to see the gunshot wound to his chest. He felt his eyes trying to tear up from the tragedy, but he stifled them back, forcing himself not to show such emotion to his men. He was still looking at his dead brother when one of the men walked over to him, standing off to the side and behind him.

"I'm sorry, Frank," the man said quietly. Although Frank did not acknowledge the condolences with words he still appreciated hearing it and managed to nod slightly.

"Where are the horses?" Frank asked, trying to move the attention away from his loss.

Another man walked up to him and was able to provide some answers. "There's several sets of reins on the ground, but it looks like two sets are missing from the team. They must have taken a couple of horses with them."

"So that means there's six of them," Frank surmised as he continued looking down at his brother. "Two horses from the team and the four of ours."

"If they only took two of the team horses where's the rest of the team?" another man who had walked over asked.

"They must have let them go," the first man answered. "Probably didn't know how long it would be before someone came along and they didn't want to take a chance that they would be stuck here and die of thirst."

"Isn't that nice?" Frank said sarcastically as he stood and faced them. "They had more compassion for some stupid horses than they did for my brother."

"Look at this," one of the men, a tall lanky man called out. "They took the guns with them."

Frank looked down to see that all of his men's guns and gun belts were missing. "Looks like they're planning on doing some shooting."

"Look over here," the tall man pointed out something else. Frank turned to see the man and a couple of others crowded around the door of the stage. His curiosity brought him over to them to see two dead men lying inside the stagecoach. He could see that both had been shot.

"Who are they?" Frank asked.

"My guess is that it's the driver and the foreman," said the tall man who had called him over.

"How can you tell?" Frank asked.

"This older one has real bad callouses on his hands from handling the reins of a team so much."

"And the other one?"

"Look at the bottom of his boots," the tall man answered. "See how theres a huge chunk worn out of the bottom next to the heel on each of his boots. That's from him rubbing them down from resting his foot on the buckboard in front of him while the stage was moving."

"So, the six that are out there are all passengers," Frank stated as he glanced around.

"Looks that way," the man responded.

"That means one of them is the one that killed Virgil," Frank pointed out.

"You don't think it could have been the driver or the foreman who did it?" another man asked.

"No," the tall man who had assessed the two dead men said. "I don't think so. That's not a shotgun wound. In fact, none of these are."

"The driver could have shot him," one man suggested.

"I doubt it. If Virgil got the drop on the the foreman before he could get off a shot with the scattergun then the driver wouldn't have had enough time to stop the stage and draw a shot," Frank stepped in to say as he turned and started for his horse.

"How can you tell he didn't fire the shotgun?"

"No empty shells," Frank turned and looked as if he was starting for his horse, but instead he walked back over to his brother and looked down at him. "Goodbye, little brother. I promise you whoever did this will pay dearly."

The rest of the men who had dismounted saw Frank

climbing into the saddle and did the same. "Which direction did they go?" he asked as he grabbed his reins.

The tall man followed the visible tracks and pointed off to the side. "Looks like they went west."

"Then that means they're headed towards Hurley," Frank said to no one in particular. "It's the nearest town besides Benton Springs."

"That's almost a three day ride," one of the men pointed out. "Why not just head into Brenton Springs?"

"Because with a rider getting away from them they knew we would be there waiting for them," Frank answered.

"Frank, I'm a fairly good tracker," the tall man admitted as he stepped into his saddle, "but I'm not good enough to follow them once they get off this main trail. Chances are, we'd lose them out there and if I did I'd probably never be able to pick it back up again. I know you don't want to chance that."

Frank Quincey hesitated briefly as he considered his options. "Stay on the trail for now so we don't lose them," he instructed the tall man as he turned to another one of his men, a younger man wearing a black hat. "Ride back into town and get the indian."

"The tracker?" the man asked trying to make sure he understood him correctly.

"Yeah," Frank responded. "Tell him we're heading west so you'll have to catch up to us." Frank turned to the tall man. "Fox, is there somewhere they can meet up with us?"

The tall man named Fox pondered the question a few seconds before answering. "By the time it'll take him to get back to town and leave with the indian and make it back here, they'll be a few hours behind us, at the very least."

"Is there anywhere they could meet us on the trail?"

"Not that I know of," Fox admitted hesitantly. "If you try to blindly pick a spot somewhere along the way you won't know if they'll end up ahead of us or behind us. We need to wait here for him to get back with the tracker."

"We aren't waiting around for nothing," Frank said to the tall man, Fox. "How far do you think you can get us?"

"I'm not sure, Frank. It depends on the terrain and how good the trail is. I'll follow it as long as I can, but then we'll have to wait for the tracker to show."

Frank nodded and then turned to the man in the black hat that he was sending back to town. "You got all of that?"

"Yeah, Frank. Get the indian and catch up with you as quick as we can. I got it," the young man with the black hat answered.

"Get going," Frank ordered the man, "and hurry." The man nodded and snatched the reins, turning his horse in the direction of town and tearing out until he was in a full gallop in a fading trail of dust.

"Riley, you and Gower bury my brother," Frank instructed as he glanced again at his brother. "Wrap him in a blanket and make sure it's plenty deep. I don't want any coyotes digging him up. By the time you're finished he should be back with the indian and then all of you can catch up with us."

"What about the rest of them?" the one called Gower asked as he pointed down to the other dead men.

"Leave 'em."

"Even our men?"

"I said leave 'em," Frank snapped as he looked at the man to further make his point. "We don't have time for you to set up a cemetery. And don't take all day, either. I need you with us." Frank turned back to the tall man, Fox. "And you're sure you can track them until the indian shows up?"

Fox nodded. "Yeah, I'll go as far as I can, Frank."

Frank Quincey pulled his horse westward, staring off into the distance. "Then start tracking."

# CHAPTER SIX

Cord Chantry led the small caravan of horses as the group traversed around the edge of a small mountain on their way to Hurley. There were plenty of ideal spots to wait out the heat of the day, but that was a luxury they could not indulge in. With men right on their tail they had to keep moving, no matter how uncomfortable the trek was turning out to be.

Although he was not overly familiar with these parts he felt he still possessed a good enough knowledge of their surroundings to get them to their destination. He had no idea how long the horses could keep up such a pace, but he couldn't worry about that right now. They would cover as much distance as they could until the horses had reached their limits and then, God forbid, they would hole up somewhere in the safest place they could find and shoot it out with Frank Quincey until one of them was dead. It wasn't the ideal plan, but at the moment it was all they had to work with.

Cord had always been the classic example of a drifter, having traversed towns all across the territory, unable, or maybe more like unwilling, to plant roots in any one spot for very long. He was a saddle tramp through and through and, as of lately, had begun to question if he was even designed for anything else. Now, at the age of twenty-seven, he had lived in a saddle more years than not, having seemingly skipped past his childhood and ending up being thrown into the role of a man far too soon. He was herding cattle by the age of ten and had started becoming proficient with a revolver just a few short years later, a skill he had felt was necessary to acquire given his circumstances.

He had never considered himself to be an expert with a gun, but he still felt as if he could hold his own if need be. His gun had proven to be the only thing he could rely on throughout his entire life and rely on it he had. But he had also learned another valuable lesson, one that was responsible for keeping him alive this far and that was that the gun was the one thing that controlled his future. If men feared it, they would respect him and leave him be, but if they chose to act according to their gun, they could be challenging and dangerous. Because of that, he preferred not to put himself in those situations and, as such, rarely frequented saloons or anywhere else that men would be drinking since drinking often led to disagreements and disagreements almost always led to guns.

Cord Chantry's demeanor was reflective of his troubled childhood. Growing up as the only child on a farm had made him strong and independent. His father had been a brutal man who obtained his rage from a bottle and dispensed it onto his own, sometimes using a small tree branch but almost always in the form of a leather belt. The beatings had been often and brutal with no one around to intervene in their savagery.

His mother had been mostly absent from his upbringing, having left their home when he was just a child, choosing instead to remain in town more than with him. She had a way with men and used that talent to be with as many of them as she wished to get what she wanted. She would periodically return to their home whenever she had fallen on hard times, which was quite frequently, and his father's love for her had ensured that he had always taken her back, although their relationship was poisonous, to say the least. Each time she returned their fighting would escalate, becoming more frequent and more violent and when she left again his anger and frustration would be taken out on young Cord.

It was for those reasons that Cord had never had what could be considered a relationship with his mother, even up to the day she was found dead in a hotel room above the saloon of a gunshot wound from her latest drunk, disgruntled date. He had never forgiven her for her actions, and her death, and had made up his mind that if he couldn't trust his own mother then he couldn't trust any other woman.

Cord had been a tall child, having reached a height of six-feet-two by age twelve and always looking older than his true age, a point that would serve him well as he left home as nothing more than an adolescent forced out into a man's world. The harsh experience of such a jagged childhood had forced him to grow up quickly and had taught him not to trust anyone with such beliefs only getting stronger as he had aged and causing him to distance himself from others as much as possible.

As he rode along, Cord glanced over at the peaks running beside them, the smell of summer blossoms filling the air as stray pieces of dandelion floated about on the soft breezes. The grass was thick and lush here, perfect for grazing and even better for game, or at least he hoped. They would need meat, and soon, judging from the meager supplies they had managed to gather before their departure, but it would have to wait until it became absolutely necessary since the firing of a rifle would most certainly give away their position to those who were, no doubt, already on their heels. Although it was a rather straight ride to Hurley, Cord didn't feel compelled to give his pursuers any more advantages than they already had.

But Frank Quincey and his men weren't his only concern. They had seen signs of bear here, mostly territorial markings on trees, probably from black bears, but possibly even coming from grizzlies. Although the grizzlies tended to stay more concealed in the trees than to remain out in the open since their immense size made it harder to remain concealed while hunting, it was still a legitimate concern. Though they feared nothing, they still reserved the right to take their prey by surprise as often as they could. That threat warranted Cord to keep an eye out for anything, at anytime.

In this country, it paid to give attention to such details since your life usually depended on it. Grizzlies were huge animals in comparison to a horse and capable of reaching a ton or more in size, but even being such a massive beast their speed was still amazing. They were able to bring down an unsuspecting horse and it's rider before they knew what was happening and often before a man could even fire a shot. Even then, a man would have to be precise at getting off a shot since they were unlikely to get a chance at a second one.

The going was slow, but steady with no one caring to engage anyone else in conversation. He supposed they all had their own ideas of how much of a chance they had of reaching the town in time and none would likely be willing to admit what they were. Two of them riding bareback complicated things even more causing Cord to hope that it wouldn't come down to an all out run for it. Clearly, no one, not even him, had any idea how far back their followers would be or what they would do when they caught up with them, although he had a pretty good idea. But none of that mattered now. They had to keep moving and put as much distance between them as possible.

He had heard too many stories about Frank Quincey, none

of which were good and most of which would make your skin crawl. The man had a reputation for being brutal, no matter if he knew the individual or not. His behavior could be explosive without warning or sometimes even without sufficient provocation. There was also the fact that he had no idea how many men Quincey had with him although the man back at the stage, Plen, had said he had twenty. He couldn't be sure if that was an accurate number or if was just a man barking threats, but there was a good chance it would be far more than what they themselves numbered.

Cord thought through their situation as he assessed those that he would be forced to fight along beside. He realized he probably wouldn't be able to count on Holbrook Sanders to help them put up a fight, doubting if the man had ever even held a gun much less used one and even if he had Cord knew the polished businessman would probably not have the courage to stand up against someone else and actually use it. But Holbrook Sanders would be helpful in reloading when, and if, it came down to a gunfight between the two groups, a likelihood that was becoming more real with each passing hour.

He had to admit that he was also somewhat concerned about Madeline Stafford. Although he couldn't exactly discount her just for being a woman he still had never been around a woman willing to fight with a gun. He didn't feel right forcing such a strong commitment onto her but, at the same time, he hoped this time she was the exception to that rule.

Madeleine had a true grit about her that other frontier women he had known did not. He had to admit that she seemed to be capable of taking care of herself, exuding a raw confidence that he admired, a confidence that would come in handy out here. She did not appear to be the type of woman to back down from a fight, even if the odds were against her.

It seemed as if she were right at home on the back of a horse and although he had no desire to put her in the middle of a gunfight he could tell he would be able to rely on her to help put up a fight when needed. The courage she had shown thus far had proven that she would not disappoint him if he needed her.

Even though he had not known Billy Richmond for very long and it seemed like he was a good kid that still wasn't enough for him to base his opinion on. Young men could appear eager when things were going well, but then suddenly choke from the pressure when their gun was needed. Cord had no way of knowing which way young Billy was going to lean and the worst of it was he would not know until the trouble had started, which was not a good time to discover if the young man could actually be counted on or not. His instincts told him that the young man probably had more fortitude than he realized.

Then there was River Holloway. There was something about the man that rubbed him the wrong way. He was a gambler, which Cord had to admit did not necessarily make him a bad person or untrustworthy, but it did make him calculating. He would be unpredictable, which in their situation could be the same as being disloyal and even dangerous. He had already expressed concern over the payroll bags twice, one of which was for not being entrusted with carrying them. Did that mean that he was hurt for not being trusted, angered for not being included or did it show his true side of just being greedy? Cord didn't know which was the case, but given their situation he was afraid he would find out at the most inopportune time. Either way, River Holloway had already proven that he was definitely someone that needed to be closely watched.

As they pressed on and all of the factors ran through his mind, Cord realized that he had a lot to consider, but even after looking at their good and bad traits there was still his greatest fear that he would not be able to count on everyone in their group when the time came to do so. They were already most definitely outnumbered and outgunned so having someone with them that could not step up to offer assistance was disheartening, to say the least.

And scary.

The horse carrying the man in the black hat bolted into town while dodging those on foot casually walking through the streets as he headed straight for the Gold Nugget Saloon. He pulled up quick, his horse almost spent from the ride, the sweat pouring off of its flanks and chest and glistening in the sun as it snorted from its exhaustion. The man didn't bother tying him to the hitching post as he was in too much of a hurry to do so. Frank Quincey was counting on him to bring the indian to him and he knew better than to disappoint the man under normal circumstances, but even more so when it came to delivering someone who would help him track down his brother's murderers.

The man flew open the batwing doors and immediately began scanning the contents of the saloon. There was a substantial crowd there, mostly made up of those seeking refuge inside from the sweltering heat and the movement of the people made it that much harder to find just one person out of the crowd. The noise was incredible, ruling out any such possibility of calling out the man's name.

He walked deeper into the building, still trying to focus on the one person he needed to find. As he moved through the crowds a man came up to him who was clearly inebriated, clumsily putting his hands on him, grabbing him and talking to him with slurred words as he tried to steady an unsteady stance. The drunkard was looking for someone to talk to, but the man with the black hat pushed him over to the side without engaging him and continued on. By the time he reached the bar, he was running out of places to look and becoming more discouraged and anxious. He took one final glance around to make sure he had not somehow missed seeing the man and decided to abandon his search as he headed for the door.

The next saloon offered no better results, nor did the third one. By the time he had arrived at the fourth saloon, he was becoming more and more desperate as the time continued ticking away. The longer it took for him to find the indian, the more distance there would be between Frank and the ones from the stage he was after. If they didn't leave soon, Frank would be even more agitated by their delay and that was not an option. Besides, he would have to change horses before they could leave as his would be unable to make the quick ride back.

He was about to abandon his search of the saloon when he caught a glimpse of someone sitting at a far table by himself. He had almost missed spotting the man in such a crowd and focused his gaze on him as he filed through the dense crowd in that direction. A man carrying two beers was pushed by the crowd and slammed into him, spilling beer all over the front of his shirt. He pushed the cowboy away, swearing out loud at the man's clumsiness.

He was still fifteen feet away when the indian spotted him and the two locked eyes. By the time the man in the black hat reached the indian's table he could see he had slid his hand down beside the table to his knife in anticipation of why the man was approaching him. The rider stopped short of the table making sure he was well out of knife range as he stared at the indian.

"Frank Quincey wants to see you."

# CHAPTER SEVEN



The man in the black hat waited for a response from the indian as his own hand lingered in the close vicinity of his gun. He dared not lose eye contact with the indian, especially in such a loud surrounding where a harsh exchange of words would be lost in such confusion and likely go unnoticed until someone lay dying on the dusty wooden floor.

He didn't know exactly what to expect from the indian, having never spent any time around him. He knew him by sight and reputation only and that was as close as he felt like getting to him. All he knew was that Frank used him because he was unquestionably the best tracker anywhere around.

The indian, Red Bear, was a Lakota warrior who had finally chosen to succumb to the invasion of the frontier settlers. He had chosen to adopt more of their lifestyle than to continue ignoring it and living with that of his own heritage, though he did not dismiss or shun it. He was a fierce man who was said to be skilled with a knife, although he was also well-known for carrying a rifle with which he was also most proficient. His steel features were such that they made him fierce enough without need of the reputation that accompanied them.

Red Bear had been named after the grizzly bear that had attacked his father while he was out in a hunting party. The attack had come out of nowhere and his father, one of the elders of the tribe, had remained at the edge of death for quite awhile and almost died from his wounds several times while his pregnant wife sat by his side, expecting the worst. When his son was born, his father had given him the name after the great beast knowing that he would grow up to be just as strong and fearless as the one who had almost cost him his own life.

Red Bear had tracked for Frank Quincey several times through the years and was a man of unequaled skill. By all accounts he was not a fan of the white settlers and chose more to avoid them than to endure their company, with Frank Quincey being the exception to the rule. Although he still frequented the saloons in town when he chose he remained more or less to himself, his staunch appearance and glaring brown eyes keeping those around him at bay.

Most of his kind would not place themselves in the midst of settlers for fear that they would be attacked or, at the very least, mistreated, but such was not the case with Red Bear. He feared no one or nothing, a fact that was well known by all of the townspeople. He knew they were to be no threat to him. They might not have liked his presence in their saloons, but they were never ignorant enough to voice that displeasure. They also knew enough about him, his past and his capabilities to know better than to try to remove him. The last man to have challenged him with a knife found himself hanging from the indian's own blade.

"Frank needs you to track some men," the man in the black hat continued as he still waited for a response. Red Bear was not known to speak the white man's language although he understood it quite well. In fact no one, including Frank Quincy himself, had ever heard the man utter any words, particularly those in english and there was question as to whether or not he even had the ability to speak, though no one ever dared to challenge him on that.

Red Bear stood from the table, sliding his knife back down into its scabbard and nodded to the man while pointing towards the saloon door, his expression flat. As the man led the indian outside, the two men drew the attention of various men along the way who eagerly stepped aside to allow them to leave. Once outside, the rider climbed up onto his horse as he waited for the indian to do the same. When they were both in their saddles, the rider led the way and the two headed over to the liver stables at a brisk walk to exchange his horse before leaving for Calhoun to get the others.

The sun was slowly creeping across the afternoon sky as Cord and the others pressed on, trying to put as many miles between them and the stagecoach as possible before they lost daylight. There was no conversation between anyone as they settled into what would hopefully be their journey to safety, if all went well, over the next few days.

Terrain was becoming denser and filled with more vegetation as they neared the hills, the mountains behind them becoming more prominent and menacing. Cord had chosen this route not because it was the easiest path to town but because it was the shortest. By cutting through the small hills they could shave off a little bit of precious time, time that might mean the difference in them making it safely to Hurley or being forced into a gunfight.

Cord noticed that there were scattered signs of animal tracks around them, an encouraging development which meant they would likely not go hungry, which was one less thing to be concerned over. The thickening terrain was a welcome sight since it also meant better shelter as well as better cover for their movements. Plus, where there was game there was water, another crucial factor they would have to be aware of and be on the lookout for.

But with all that preoccupied his mind he still felt a deep sense of guilt. He felt bad that they had not taken the time to bury the stage driver and the foreman, but given their circumstances time simply had not permitted it. Someone would be along soon, he kept telling himself to try to ease his conscience, another stage perhaps and they could notify those in the next town of their discovery. Still, the thought gave him little solace. It was not the way he liked to see a man go out, especially an innocent one that had fallen because of the actions of a dishonest man, but he felt he had no other choice. As for the robbers, he had left it up to Frank Quincey to take care of his own men.

With a large group of men breathing down his neck they couldn't risk being out in the open when Quincey caught up with them, a risk that would be nothing short of suicide if they were to catch up to them before they reached sufficient cover. They had to make it to the hills to at least give themselves somewhat of a fighting chance, if there was, in fact, any chance at all. He would never admit it to the others but he had his doubts that they would even make it to Hurley in time. Despite his doubts he decided that there was already enough tension in the group without adding something more that none of them could do anything about. His only option was to keep moving and hope the distance they already had between them would continue to grow, or at the very least, not fade too quickly.

They continued pushing on the rest of the afternoon without incident, taking great care not to push the horses too hard, too quickly. The best scenario would have been to limit riding during the hottest times of the day and to save their horses' energy for the cooler times of the evening, but that luxury was not an option for them since he knew Quincey would be bearing down on them.

Cord noticed that Madeline and Holbrook Sanders hadn't uttered a word since the group had left the stagecoach, but several times he stole a glance at River and noticed the man was eyeing him as if there were something in the back of his mind that was annoying him. Cord couldn't put his finger on exactly what it was that bothered him, but something about the man did not sit well with him. While Madeline and Holbrook, or even Billy Richmond for that matter, didn't warrant extra attention the same couldn't be said for River Holloway.

He questioned the man's sense of loyalty, wondering just how far the man was willing to go to protect the group. Was he really a team player or was that just a facade that he showed to them as a way to buy his time before he made his move, a move that was surely not to be in their best interest? He would need to remember to tell Nathan and Madeline to help keep an eye on River, just in case.

The sun was making its final appearance in the sky as evening started descending upon them. The combination of the prolonged heat and the wear of the ride had taken its toll on them, draining them both physically and mentally. The air was already starting to cool even before the sun slipped down low enough to touch the horizon as it ushered in the lower temperatures of the upcoming night. They settled on a spot next to the trees that offered them a clear vantage point of anyone coming up through the valley, hopefully taking away Frank Quincy's element of surprise.

There was plenty of grass here and the greener vegetation and various type of tracks suggested there was some source of water nearby. Normally, the trail would be dotted with small pockets of water but this time of year those sources would be limited. Thankfully, they had remembered to take the canteens of the driver and the foreman. Even with adding them with the ones from the robber's horses their water intake would still have to be rationed, just in case.

Cord and Billy volunteered to go in search of water and food while Nathan and the rest of the group began to set up a simple camp with a small fire with little glow so as not to attract attention. Just as Cord and the young man were about to leave, Nathan motioned with his head for Cord to come over to him. They walked a few yards away from the camp for privacy.

"What's up?" Cord asked him.

"For the last hour or so I've had this feeling that someone is watching us."

The comment caught Cord by surprise and concern as he was generally accustomed to picking up such uneasiness. "Have you seen anything?"

"No, it's just a feeling. But I can't seem to shake it."

"You're probably just getting anxious over Quincey and his men, that's all."

"Yeah, I hope so. It's just a nagging feeling."

"I haven't seen anything, but I'll let Billy know to keep an eye out, too. Probably shouldn't say anything to the others, though, at least until we have more to go on or else it might get 'em spooked."

Nathan nodded as they turned and headed back over to the fire, although the thought still lingered in Cord's mind. Nathan wasn't the type of man to be put on edge like that. He hoped the man was just making up the uneasiness because of their pursuers, but, at the same time, he couldn't discount his concern since they couldn't be too careful out here. This newest matter coupled with the threat of Frank Quincey made it almost certain that tonight he was going to be in for a restless night of sleep.

It was clear that the horses were spent and deserved a much needed rest, especially since no one knew how hard they had been ridden before the botched robbery took place so they felt it best to err on the side of caution. Should it become necessary for them to make a run for it, the last thing they needed was exhausted horses to slow down or even halt their escape completely.

Cord knew that Frank Quincey was the type of man who would never take the welfare of his horses into consideration. He would be willing to push them past their limit until they dropped dead and then take off in pursuit on foot, if necessary. He had too much hatred festering inside of him to care about anything other than exacting vengeance. For that reason, Cord felt it was better to get an early start long before daylight to not only take advantage of the cooler temperatures but to save the horses as much as possible.

Before leaving their camp, Cord had made sure to leave the bags of money in Madeline and Nathan's care, reminding them to keep an eye out for River in their absence. The two of them noticed that River still had his gun and gun belt they had taken off of the robbers and even, at one point, had considered taking it from him. But, in the end, they felt his needing it in the event that Frank Quincey caught up with them outweighed the risk of him using it against them to try to steal the money. Besides, River had no knowledge of the area or of living off the land and would likely end up succumbing to exposure or animals, and possibly even Quincey himself, before he could make it to town on his own.

When Nathan decided to go hunt for firewood he pulled Madeline over to the side just out of the hearing of River. He could tell the man was watching his every move but he didn't care. It was evident from his soured expression that he already had a good idea what Nathan was telling her, that he wasn't to be trusted.

Holbrook sat by the growing fire and worked on trying to remove some of the trail from his jacket with his handkerchief that it had picked up during their ordeal. Although Nathan still knew very little about Holbrook, he dismissed him as being any sort of a threat. Holbrook wasn't the one that he nor Cord was concerned about.

"I'm going to get some more wood," Nathan advised her quietly as he cut his eyes over to River. "Keep your gun out where you can get to it fast, if you need it."

"I'll be alright," Madeline answered with a nod as she shifted the gun closer to her body.

"Would you like some help, Mr. Brooks?" Holbrook asked with a slight grin. "I don't feel I'm of much use just sitting around the fire."

"It's 'Nathan'," he answered, "and, yeah, I can always use the help."

"Wonderful," the man responded as he laid his jacket over a log and followed Nathan out of the camp. River watched the two men until they were out of sight before he threw Madeline a shrewd smile.

"I don't think your friend Cord likes me very much," he stated in a casual drawl as he stood and began slowly walking around the fire closer to her. Being there alone with him, his movement made her uneasy, but she remembered the gun and placed her hand closer to it without trying to draw attention to it.

"I know Nathan told you to keep an eye on me," River continued. He started to step around Holbrook's bedding which was the one closest to Madeline, but she reached down for the gun without taking her eyes off of him. Her reaction caused him to stop as he held up his hands. "There's no need for you to go for your gun, madam," he tried assuring her. "I am not an idiot. I know you are likely to shoot me if I try anything." He sat down on the log where Holbrook had laid his jacket. "Is this better?"

Madeline didn't respond, but she did ease her hand slightly away from the gun as she watched him carefully. "Why do you think that is?" she asked, her look steely and fixed.

"Why do I think what is?" he responded.

"Why do you think Cord doesn't like you?"

River shrugged. "That, I do not know. I have not done anything to him nor given him cause for distrust. Perhaps he has been out on the range by himself too long and no longer trusts anyone."

"Or maybe it's because you tried to get him to leave Nathan behind at the stagecoach," she corrected him.

"Oh, yes, there was that," River said sarcastically with a smile. "I'm sorry but I did not mean it, my dear. Rather, I was just speaking in the moment."

Calling her by that title made her feel uncomfortable. "Well, Cord thought you meant it."

"I'm afraid your Mr. Chantry is not always a good judge of character," River surmised with a smile. "He doesn't really know anything about any of us, now does he? Besides, you have to admit he doesn't appear to be warming up much to you, either."

"He may just be that he's not comfortable around women."

"Or perhaps there is something unpleasant in Mr. Chantry's past concerning a woman."

"That's none of our concern."

"Well, regardless, I'm just as anxious to get into town as the rest of you. What reason would I have to jeopardize that way out here in the middle of nowhere?"

"I can think of twenty-seven-thousand reasons," she pointed out flatly, her eyes unwavering.

The frankness of her comment cut him deeply as his demeanor changed to a colder version. "But you must remember that it is not his money, either," River stated harshly. "You must understand that I simply pointed out the obvious. For all the railroad knows that money was stolen by Frank Quincey's gang. He's going to get blamed for it anyway so what exactly is the harm?"

"The *harm* is that it's not our money."

He studied her with cool contempt. "Cord says that now, but money has a way of changing men, my dear lady. You have him labeled as being an honorable man, but I assure you that he is not. In my travels I've seen it happen with many men and Cord is no different."

"Yes, he is. He wouldn't change like that."

"Sooner or later, he will come to his senses and realize what he has. They all do," River said as he stood and walked back over to his bedding. "Wait and see."

# CHAPTER EIGHT

The faint sound of running water slowed Cord and Billy's movements as they hesitated in their tracks, straining to pinpoint its origin. They determined that the sound was coming from in front of them, that was for certain, but the sight of it was obscured by trees and bushes. Even as anxious as they were to find water they dared not rush into an unfamiliar area without checking it out first. Other creatures would likely also be looking for water, some of which they would not care to cross paths with.

Billy started to pass through the brush, but Cord reached over and grabbed his arm before he could do so, stopping the young man in his tracks. When he looked over at Cord, Cord placed his finger to his lips to quiet his movements, alerting him to stay back as if he knew something the young man did not. Billy nodded in compliance and waited for Cord to lean in closer and carefully spread the limbs of the bush in front of them. The two men looked through the limbs to see a buck drinking from a small creek less than a hundred feet away, casually flicking its tail as it enjoyed the cool water. It was a large animal with a massive rack of antlers, the type that any hunter would relish as a trophy and would love to have adorn the wall of their home. But as impressive as the animal's rack was, they would not be able to put it to use this time for this was strictly a matter of survival.

Cord slowly released the limbs allowing them to fold back to their original position and motioned for Billy to slowly sit down the canteens he had been carrying in the grass. He lifted his rifle and slowly eased the barrel straight through the limbs until it was clear of the bush while he carefully pulled the lever back to load a cartridge, anticipating the clicking sound it would make while doing so. As it chambered the round, the sound caused Cord to stop his movement and glance through the bush. The buck was put on high alert, raising its head from drinking, it's ears pricked and at attention as it sought to locate where the sound had come from.

The two men waited, each being absolutely motionless and each silently hoping the sound had not been enough to alarm the deer and cause it to sprint for the nearest cover. The seconds seemed to drag on forever as they sat quietly watching and waiting. Finally convinced it was not in any danger, the deer settled down and lowered its head to take in another drink. Cord closed one eye, took careful aim and fired, the bullet striking the buck squarely in the side and causing its body to stiffen as it took a clumsy half step towards the water and fell down into the creek.

"You got him!" Billy yelled with laughter. "That was a good shot!"

"Well, at least we won't starve," Cord said as he stood and walked around the bush towards the fallen deer. Billy looked down at it smiling while admiring Cord's skill with a rifle.

"That was a clean shot through the heart," the young man exclaimed. "You knew right where to hit him."

Cord handed the canteens to Billy. "Here. You fill these and I'll start dressing it."

The two went to work, each at their own task without talking. Cord drew a hunting knife from his boot and started to work on the deer, making precise cuts as if born to the trade as he carved out specific pieces of meat. By the time Billy had filled all of the canteens, Cord had already carved out several large sections of meat and was wrapping it in a shirt he had brought with him. Cord hated having to be forced into firing a weapon out here knowing that if Frank Quincey was within hearing distance he would now know exactly where they were. His only hope was that they were still out of range and that the dense trees muffled the sound enough to mask it.

"We'll have to keep an eye out tonight back at camp," Cord warned Billy. "That deer carcass is going to bring every animal in the area down here to feed off of it. Probably wouldn't be a bad idea to post a lookout to make sure none of them happen to wander into camp, too, especially while we're sleeping."

"Sounds good," Billy said with a nod.

As they took their goods and started back towards camp Cord tried to push Nathan's warning out of his mind, but it lingered and irritated him like a burr under a saddle. The thought that someone might be following them wasn't likely, but the man's concern had been genuine and this was no place to simply dismiss a warning even if it was nothing more than a feeling. The only ones that should be following them were Quincey and his men. But he had to admit that the thought of someone else already being out here was quite plausible.

The area was prime for trapping and there were even some rumors of old mines around the area that might not have been played out. Then there were always those who were just passing through for whatever the reason. Regardless, one thing was for certain. They would need to do a better job of hiding the money bags when they got back to camp, just in case someone did wander up on them.

When they arrived back at camp, Nathan and River had gathered some rocks and small tree limbs and stacked them on the side facing back towards the stagecoach in order to try to block the glow of the fire as much as possible from those following. It was a relatively clear view down the valley for quite a distance, far enough that a fire, no matter how small, could be detected. They didn't need to give away their location in the event that Quincey continued riding through the night, which was a distinct possibility.

Cord had pushed the horses as far as he had felt comfortable before stopping just short of the first range of hills that could be considered small mountains. The going would be slower once they touched the base of those hills, but it was still the better option to give them as much of a fighting chance as possible. His hope was that Quincey would take the bait and continue on around the mountains, unknowingly opening up their lead even more, but he knew that was a long shot.

It took virtually no time for Nathan to have the venison steaks cooking on top of some large flat rocks over the fire. As the sizzle of the meat filled the night air, Cord walked over to where he was squatting and monitoring their progress, his stomach growled and his mouth watering from the enticing aroma. "Have you had any more feelings like someone is trailing us?"

"Yeah, they're still there. I hope I'm wrong, but I've been keeping an eye out just in case I'm not."

"I set Billy up just over that last rise to watch the trail behind us. He'll be able to see anyone coming in enough time to give us some warning. Since it's already dark, after we eat I'll take the first watch. I want to be on the trail again long before sunup. I've got a feeling that Quincey is really going to be pushing down on us hard tomorrow."

"You mean skip breakfast so we can get an earlier start?" Nathan asked as he turned a couple of the steaks.

"I think we need to. We've got to do whatever we have to in order to say ahead of him. If it comes down to a shootout, we won't stand a chance. What do you think?"

"I agree."

"I'll tell Holbrook, Billy and Madeline."

"What about River?"

"I want to keep him out of the loop, at least for now. The less he knows about what we have planned, the better I'll feel."

"You don't think he would try something, do you?"

"I don't know. I wouldn't put it past him."

"What'd you do with the money bags?"

"They're stuffed down between my saddle and the log it's propped up against," Cord informed him quietly. "I told Billy where they were so he could sit around the fire and keep an eye on them."

"Did River see you put them there?"

"No, I waited until he had walked away from camp to do it. But I'm sure he's wondering where they are."

"You're really worried about him, aren't you?"

"You should be, too."

"Why is that?"

"Because he wanted to leave you behind at the stagecoach."

Nathan gave Cord a surprised glance. He had not expected to hear such a thing. "Are you serious?"

"Yep. He got mad when I told him 'no'. Everybody was standing around and heard it."

Nathan shook his head as if in disbelief. "What about Madeline?"

"She won't say anything. She doesn't care for him in the least. We've just got to keep his hands off of those bags until we can make it to Hurley. I'll be glad when we get there so I won't have to worry about them anymore."

A short while later, everyone except Billy was sitting within close proximity of the fire dining on venison steak. "Get your fill," Cord warned them. "It'll probably be the last big meal we get till we reach town." He hurriedly polished off his meal and had picked up his rifle. "I'm going to relieve Billy so he can come eat," he announced to Nathan and Madeline, who were sitting next to one another. "If you hear me fire a gunshot, get on your horses and get out of here immediately. Head straight for the notch over there," he said as he pointed off into the distance where a notch had been carved out of the hillside, clearly visible from the glow of the half-moon lighting up the clear sky. "Thread that notch and stay straight and it'll take you directly..."

He halted his instructions, his body suddenly tensed as he waited. *A noise.* He quietly glanced at Nathan, who looked over at him and nodded. *He heard it, too.* Nathan slowly put down his plate and stood, grabbing his rifle in the process, each man taking a glimpse of their surroundings, their breathing shallow, their ears perched and ready for any sound that would point to a direction.

Cord slowly pulled his revolver with his free hand and waited. The sound of a twig crunching underfoot sent both men spinning around into the direction of the sound behind them with Cord cocking his gun while Nathan chambered a round in his rifle. They waited, their eyes focused on the darkness beyond them, their senses perched on the edge of action when a man's voice called out.

"You in the camp. Can I come in?"

"Who are you?" Cord asked as he pointed his gun in the man's direction.

"My name's Tell. Tell Witherspoon. And don't worry, mister. I ain't no troublemaker. Honest. I'm just passing through."

"Come out where we can see you," Cord ordered the man, "and don't try anything. There's two guns on you."

A few seconds later, they heard the bushes being parted as a man slowly walked into the camp, his hands held up for them to see. He stopped just inside the bushes where they could get a better look at him. "That's far enough," Cord instructed him. "Where'd you come from?"

"A ways back in the woods. I've got to be honest with 'ya, mister, I didn't have anything to eat and I was about to settle down for the night when I thought I smelled your cooking. Wouldn't mind having some of whatever it is you're making, if you don't mind. At this point I don't even care what it is. I'd be much obliged."

Cord looked the young man over. He was around Billy's age and was wearing a gun that was tied down. He looked sincere, and hungry. "You alone, Tell?"

"Yessir, have been since I left Bakersville."

"Where 'ya headed?" Cord asked, feeling somewhat better about the visitor though his guard was still up.

"Don't really know. Wherever the land takes me, I guess."

"Probably not a good idea for you to be out here by yourself. Too many things to get into."

"Mister, I don't mind talking to you, but I ain't ate since yesterday. You mind if I get something to eat and then we can talk?"

Cord glanced over at Nathan who gave him a simple nod as he continued covering the stranger with his rifle. Cord doubted the man would try anything when he could clearly see that everyone there was armed, including Madeline, but he wasn't taking any chances. "Drop your gun belt and come on in."

Tell Witherspoon eagerly unbuckled his gun belt and dropped it onto the ground as he made a straight shot for the fire. When Nathan glanced over, Cord motioned to him to circle the camp, looking for anyone else who might be with Tell. Meanwhile, Cord was in the process of pulling a venison steak off the fire and putting it on a plate when the young man walked over to him and waited, licking his lips in anticipation of the meal. When Cord handed him the plate he was reaching for a fork to give him but Tell grabbed the hunk of meat before he could and took a huge bite out of it. He closed his eyes as he chewed vigorously. "Ummm...that's so good. You really know how to cook a steak, mister."

Cord sat down across from the young man and was watching him devour his food. "So, Tell, how long have you been out here?"

"More than a week...wait...what day is it?"

"Tuesday."

Tell nodded as he bit off another chunk of meat. "Yeah, more'n a week."

"Seen anybody else since you got out here?"

"Nope. Saw some bear, but that was about it. I was just hoping I didn't see any Lakota."

Cord poured himself a cup of coffee and was blowing on it to try to cool it when Nathan walked over, nodding his head in agreement that it looked as if Tell was alone. "What kind of work do you do, Tell?"

The young man had to wait to swallow his latest mouthful before he could answer. "Mostly ranch hand, but I have been on a cattle drive."

"Well, I'm headed to a friend's ranch to help him work the place. I'm sure he could use another hand, if you're interested."

Tell's expression lit up from the offer. "Yeah, I'm interested! Thanks, mister."

"Cord."

"Well, thanks, Cord! Where's the job?"

"Hurley."

"I've never been there before. When do we leave?"

"Before daylight. Probably be on the road by five or maybe a little after."

The young man threw Cord a curious look. "Why so early?"

Cord glanced over at Nathan. "We're in kind of a hurry to get there."

# CHAPTER NINE

The small team of men led by Frank Quincey pulled up to a stop under a grove of trees, their horse snorting and stomping about as they tried to calm down from the exertion that was just required of them. They had been hot on Cord's trail for several hours, not knowing whether or not they were making any progress. Frank was prepared to continue pushing but he could tell the horses had pretty much reached their limit for the day. The heat had taken its toll on them so he decided against pushing them any further since he needed them to be ready for tomorrow. The last thing they needed was to be stranded out here without enough horses.

Quincey walked over to the tall man, Fox, a frown gathered between his eyes. He didn't like the pace they were keeping. It felt as if they weren't making any progress, although he had no way of knowing for sure if that were the case. He was letting his emotions in the situation get the better of him, he knew that, and for that, he wasn't thinking clearly. All he knew was he wanted to get to Virgil's killers, wanted it more than anything else he had ever wanted in his entire life and he meant to have it. He needed to take something away from them like what they took from him.

"Any sign of them?" he asked Fox.

"They're still laying down a good trail, but I don't know how much longer it'll last. I can follow them for now, but at any time they could disappear."

"I wonder if Lee is on his way back with the indian," Quincey said in general as he rubbed the coarse bristle of hair on his chin. Things weren't happening fast enough for him and he had no way to change that. The inability to control the situation was not something he was accustomed to and it annoyed him greatly. "We've got to make up more time," Quincey pointed out as he scanned the hills before him, hoping to get a glimpse of the fugitives scurrying away.

"We're already pushing the horses as much as we dare," Fox pointed out reluctantly. He knew how much disappointment Frank Quincey could take, how much he would be willing to take before he lost his composure and it felt as if that limit was rapidly approaching. The thought of what he, Quincey, would do, to him in particular if he failed to deliver these people to him was not something he cared to dwell on. He had witnessed Quincy's rage before and the last thing he wanted was to witness it again, specifically if it were directed at him.

"We've got to move faster,' Quincey announced as he looked at him in his disgust.

Fox hated to point out the obvious, but he felt he needed to in order to offer a warning in the event that something happened. "We'll kill the horses."

"Then, we'll kill 'em!" Quincey snapped, all the while knowing his logic made no sense but realizing he couldn't back down. He abruptly turned away and walked over to the small mesa that bordered them, scaling its side for a better view of what lay ahead. Once he was up there, he glanced in their intended direction looking for something, anything, that would give away the position of his prey, but saw nothing. They were still too far back, a half-day behind, perhaps less. And at some point the trail would become too faint for Fox to be able to pick up. Then what? Sit and wait for the indian? It would be a waste of time, but there was nothing he could do about it. The realization angered him.

If he allowed these people to reach Hurley, they would have refuge, a town to use for cover and the law to hide behind. He would have no chance at justice there. Although the law around Benton Springs had always been hesitant to try to bring him in he could not say the same for Hurley, having only ventured there once. Hurley was bigger and more modern than Benton Springs and once there he had only his reputation working in his favor. If the law was as solid as in other larger towns it would receive the backing of the townspeople. Such towns would not allow he and his men to come in and take over the place like he had Benton Springs. These towns had rules in place and he would be required to follow those rules, something he had never been good at doing. No, he had to catch these people before then.

The darkness had completely fallen over them when Quincey scanned the expansive range looking for signs of a fire. Surely they would have made one since the nights were still too chilly without one. The terrain was such that he could still see a far distance but there was nothing. Frustrated, he climbed down from the mesa and walked over to their camp, ignoring the silent glances his men were giving him. He squatted next to the fire, holding his hands out to take in its warmth as he slowly rubbed away the chill from them. Once he had sufficiently rubbed away enough of the cold he picked up a cup and filled it with coffee, cupping it in his hands to take advantage of the heat the liquid generated.

He was lost in thought when a voice from behind him interrupted his thoughts.

"Any luck, Frank?" one of the men asked. "I saw you up on the mesa looking out."

Quincey did not turn towards him but continued staring into the fire. "No. Just an empty valley."

"Me and some of the boys we're talking," the man continued. "We were wondering what we were going to do if we didn't catch up with them before they made it to Hurley."

"We keep going until we do."

"Frank, do you know who the sheriff is in Hurley? It's Sage Connelly."

Frank Quincey threw the name around in his mind. He had heard of the man. He was known as a stern enforcer of the law and for keeping the peace in his town. Last he had heard, Connelly was the sheriff down in Compton, once a ruthless atmosphere where killing had become commonplace and lawlessness was widespread. The previous sheriff of Compton had been murdered while making his rounds one fateful night, but no one had ever been brought to justice. Stories abounded that there were no witnesses. Others claimed there were but they were too scared of retaliation to come forward. Either way, the law had been erased and no one of reasonable caliber had been willing to take over such a dangerous post.

Sage Connelly had stepped in and had done just that, his reputation having become such that the town had finally relaxed and accepted it's renewed freedom. And if the rumors were true then Connelly wasn't the type of man to let Frank Quincey and his men come in and take that away from him. He wouldn't hesitate to put up a fight, no doubt with plenty of the townspeople to back him. That meant only one thing. They had to get Virgil's killers before they made it to Hurley.

"What if we don't catch up with them before they make it

into town?" the man asked as if reading Frank Quincy's thoughts.

"Then we'll go in there after them," Quincey resigned, his tone calm while still trying to disguise his concern. "I'm not going to let some sheriff stop me."

"But Hurley isn't like Benton Springs," the man pointed out as two other men wandered up behind him to listen in on the growing conversation. "The law won't touch you back there, but Hurley isn't like that."

"I know it isn't like that," Quincey stated bluntly as he stood abruptly, staring at the cluster of men. He scanned the faces of the others around the fire, checking them for resistance all the while knowing that they were probably silently questioning his logic. "If it comes to it, we'll ride into Hurley and take it over like we did Benton Springs. The townspeople will be too afraid to pick up a gun when we hit town with twenty men. The people who killed Virgil aren't going to be able to hide out there, or anywhere else, for that matter, no matter who they try to hide behind. I'll turn over every rock and search every canyon from here to Hurley and anywhere else I need to until I find them. I'll burn Hurley to the ground, kill anyone that gets in my way and walk over their dead bodies if need be, but I'm going to find the ones responsible for killing my brother and kill every last stinking one of 'em!"

Having polished off her latest cup of coffee, Madeline Stafford stood and walked over to the fire, pouring another cup from the blackened pot more to help warm her up than for the taste, savoring the aroma and the warmth to her hands. She delicately sipped it while staring at Cord who was just about to head out for his watch and was sitting on the log closest to the fire, quiet and apparently deep in thought. She casually walked over and sat down next to him.

"Still no sign of them? " she asked, knowing he was aware of who she was referring to.

"No," Cord said as he glanced back at nothing on their trail and then returned his gaze to the fire.

"You don't talk very much, do you, mister Chantry? Or is it that you don't particularly want to talk to *me?*"

"It's nothing personal."

"Well, it feels personal."

Cord sighed into an explanation. "I've just never had much luck with the women in my life."

"An old flame?"

"My mother, for one," he hesitantly admitted. "And there were others."

"What kind of others?"

"It doesn't matter. Just drop it."

"Oh, okay."

Cord's uneasiness at the subject caused him to divert the conversation elsewhere. "I wish I knew just how far back Quincey was. The not knowing is what's bugging me. At least out here I'd have some time to react, but this uncertainty, this is driving me nuts."

Madeleine felt his uneasiness, but there was nothing she could do to help settle his mind. Cord was quiet, his manner was easy and completely confident but he was still worried. She knew his type, a man who was not accustomed to worrying. He never wanted to show his emotions on his sleeve but he also had to be realistic about the situation that they were in. She knew he was trying to hold it together for her, for them, but the doubt was still leaking through. She could see him struggling with the facts. She decided to try to take his mind off of things, at least for the time being. Her thoughts went back to the stagecoach. "Why were you staring at me at the stagecoach station?"

The comment served its purpose and brought Cord out of his thoughts. "*What?*"

"Back at the stagecoach station. I saw you staring at me for quite some time. Surely you've seen women out here before."

"Yeah, I guess."

"Well, I'm no different than any of them."

"Not every woman is pretty."

"Surely you've seen pretty women in your travels."

Cord answered her without looking up. "Not as pretty as you." The words spilled from his lips even before he was aware he was saying them. He had lowered his guard and she had gotten in. He cursed silently to himself at the comment.

Madeline sat quietly, stunned at the confusion as she took in his comment. "So you think I'm pretty?"

He suddenly caught himself for what he had said. "Sure," he said and then briefly hesitated. "What man wouldn't?"

She was flattered and yet surprised that he had opened up to her. "I suppose some men have thought me pretty, but I never really knew if it was because they thought it was true or if they were only interested in me because I was a woman."

"Maybe its both."

Madeleine wasn't exactly sure how to take his response so she decided to see it as a compliment. Men like Cord had difficulty speaking how they felt, especially to a woman, so she took his confession as proof that he was interested in her. Though flattered she still wasn't exactly sure how she felt about it. She knew nothing of the man nor what he was capable of, a thought that somewhat scared her. Till now he had managed to keep the peace and had even gotten them out of the holdup without incident. He had taken charge and gotten them this far. But what would happen when he realized how much money they were carrying? River had pointed it out to her about how money had a way of changing men, of bringing out their worst side and twenty-seven-thousand dollars was an awful lot of money to ignore. She felt as if he wouldn't be tempted by such an amount, but, then again, she had to admit to herself that she also had her doubts.

"You were right about River," she said out of the blue.

"How's that?"

"He tried to convince me that you were interested in the money. Said your true feelings would come out and you'd end up taking the money."

"It's not my money."

"I know, but he said it didn't matter."

"I made a promise to the driver that I would get it back to the sheriff and that's what I'm going to do."

"He tried to convince me to take the money with him. He said it would be the perfect cover since Frank Quincey would be blamed for it anyway."

"And what do you think?"

"I couldn't do it. Like you said, it isn't our money."

"River is the one that deserves to be watched."

"I agree," she said flatly while still faintly smiling. "But you have to admit it is a lot of money. Tell the truth. Aren't you just a little bit tempted?"

"No," Cord answered sharply as he stood and walked over towards the horses. She watched him until he was out of sight, unable to see the look of disgust smeared on his face as she glanced back at the fire, frustrated at what she had done. She had wanted him to open up to her, but instead she had managed to accomplish the one thing she hadn't wanted. She had pushed too far and insulted him.

She had pushed him away.

# CHAPTER TEN

The man with the badge looked down at the scene before him, puzzled and trying to piece together exactly what had happened. His appearance at the stagecoach had been prompted by a telegram from the sheriff in Benton Springs wondering why the morning stage had not arrived in his town, something that had never happened before. Even the few times the stage had been robbed it was still able to limp into town afterwards. It's failure to appear had the sheriff and the bank worried.

The inquiry into the missing stage had peaked the sheriff's interest enough to have him grab his deputy and a man from town who was known for his tracking skills and head out on the path of the stagecoach which was a straight shot on the road from Jackson Creek to Benton Springs. The search party of three had made it well more than halfway to Benton Springs when they came upon it.

The stagecoach was sitting in the middle of the road, it's door open and baggage strewn about as if someone had been pilfering through it. Lying just inside on the floor of the stagecoach was the driver and the foreman, both shot at close range and both dead. There were three other bodies lying there next to the stagecoach, none of which he recognized and none of which had their guns or gun belts, which he thought was odd. Their horses were also gone along with two of the horses from the stagecoach team. Even before he looked he knew the payroll bags would be missing. The scene was bewildering and out of place and raised so many questions that he didn't know where to begin.

All three men climbed down and began processing what they were seeing. Sheriff Jonathan Peck walked slowly around the bodies trying to piece together a reasonable explanation but, so far, nothing made any sense.

"What do you think happened here, sheriff?" asked a man assisting the sheriff as he looked down at the bodies, equally puzzled at the sight.

Sheriff Peck pondered the scene as he took in all of the details. In his eleven years as a peace office he had never seen anything even remotely similar to what he was looking at now. "Looks like a robbery gone bad," he finally declared. "The only thing I can't understand is where are these men's horses? And why is a pair of the team also missing?"

One of them, the man not wearing a badge, walked over to the sheriff. "I found several sets of tracks over on the other side of the stage."

"What are they?" he asked as he stepped over to the man.

"This first set of tracks are fresh ones and there's a lot of them. They're heading out through the valley.

"How many are we talking about?"

"At least four or five, maybe even more. It's hard to say with so many hoof marks. Then, there's another set right next to it."

"How many in the second group?"

The man studied the prints a few seconds before answering. "Five, maybe six horses. I traced two of them over to the stagecoach team. That's where your two lead horses ended up."

"And they're all headed out through the valley, too?"

"Yessir, sheriff. I also followed this set of tracks," the tracker pointed down at the markings at their feet, "and they lead over there to a grave."

"A *grave?*" Sheriff Peck questioned. "Are you sure it's a grave?"

"Yeah, I'm sure, sheriff," the deputy answered. "Can't be more than a day old, if that."

"That doesn't make any sense. Who buries a body way out here? And why would anyone even take the time to dig a grave in the first place? Why not just bring them back to town for a proper burial?"

The deputy pondered the issue for a few seconds before offering his take on it. "Maybe whoever held up the stage forced the passengers to bury someone. Maybe one of the passengers?"

"Robbers wouldn't waste the time doing that," the deputy stated. "Besides, they could care less if someone got shot, much less take the time and decency to bury them."

Sheriff Peck shook his head. "He's right, that doesn't make sense. These guys," he added as he pointed down at the dead men on the ground, "are the ones that held up the stage. If they're all dead then they wouldn't be around to demand something like taking the time to dig a grave. They would be too concerned with taking the money and getting away. Besides, who would they be burying?"

"Dunno, sheriff, but it's definitely a fresh grave."

Sheriff Peck pondered the situation further, but couldn't come up with a reasonable explanation that would answer all of his questions. He abandoned his questions while he went to something that could be answered. "What time did the stage leave this morning?"

"Ten o'clock, right on schedule," the third man, the tracker, declared.

"How many people were on board?"

"It was full," the deputy said as he looked over the bodies. "I think there was six, not counting the driver and the foreman."

Sheriff Peck briefly ran the logic through his mind. He had to assume that the dead men outside of the stage were the robbers, or at least some of them. Their horses were gone, as were two of the team. Six horses. Six riders. That would make sense. But who were the riders of the six horses that they talking about? Was it the passengers? And if it was the passengers, where exactly did they go?

"Do we know anything about the passengers? Anything that would cause them to stand out?"

"Not really," the deputy answered. "Fella at the stage office said they all looked just like ordinary travelers."

"Were any of them traveling together?"

"Don't think so. He didn't mention anything like that."

The layout of things had Sheriff Peck at a loss. The way it looked the travelers were held up, the robbers were all killed, one of which was then buried and then the passengers took all of the horses and left with the money. As if that wasn't strange enough the passengers didn't go back to town, or even the stagecoach station, not that it would have done them any good to do so since there was no law there. Sheriff Peck was the law in Jackson Creek and would have noticed if a group of six strangers rode into town, two of them on large black Shires without saddles. Even if they had managed to slip past him they couldn't have made it into town without at least someone noticing. That kind of a group were definitely bound to draw attention from someone.

"Do you think they headed into Benton Springs?" the

deputy asked while brandishing the same puzzled expression as the sheriff.

"No, I don't think so. Frank Quincey pretty much runs Benton Springs. Everyone knows that. No one would be stupid enough to pull off a robbery in his back yard without getting his approval. He'd kill anyone who tried to do that just for suggesting it."

"Maybe it *was* Frank Quincey," the deputy suggested.

"I doubt it," the sheriff closed down the notion. "He wouldn't have sent just four men, especially four men that would have a chance of failing at a robbery. His men don't make a move without his say-so. None of them would have botched this job."

"Well, if they didn't come back to Jackson Creek and they didn't go into Benton Springs, then where are they?"

"Sheriff!" the man who discovered the grave called out. Sheriff Peck walked around the stage to the far side facing the valley where the man was standing looking down at something on the ground.

"I could follow these tracks for awhile, if you want, but I'd be willing to bet they're headed to Hurley."

Sheriff Peck looked off in the direction of Hurley. "So the passengers took the money and hightailed it through the valley to the only town anywhere near that direction, which is Hurley. But that still doesn't answer why they rode off instead of waiting here for help to come."

"Maybe they didn't have time to wait," the deputy responded.

"Maybe they were afraid to wait," Sheriff Peck corrected.

The deputy nodded. "Either way, it looks like they were after the payroll."

"You're saying six random passengers bought tickets, loaded up on the stage, got out here in the middle of nowhere, got robbed, killed all of the robbers, stole the horses and then rode off with the payroll? I don't buy it. It doesn't make sense."

"What part of it doesn't make sense?" the deputy asked.

"If you're trying to get away with a payroll, why take the time to bury one of the robbers? Why just one? Why not all of them? And why bury this one in particular? Why him over anyone else?"

"I don't know, sheriff," the deputy responded, clearly confused by the sheriff's points. "I know it doesn't really make sense, but people do strange things for that much money."

Sheriff Peck glanced over at the deputy. "How much money are we talking about here?"

"The fella at the bank said a little over twenty-seven thousand dollars."

"That's a lot of money. Why would they have that kind of money on them?"

"The fella at the bank said it was the railroad and the mining payrolls combined."

Sheriff Peck started to turn back towards the stage when the man doing the tracking stopped him. "Wait, sheriff, there's something else."

"What is it?" Sheriff Peck asked as he turned back around.

"There's more tracks over here," the man said as he walked a few yards over and pointed down at the ground.

Sheriff Peck walked over to where the man was motioning. "How many tracks?"

"A set of two."

"Okay, so who do those belong to?"

"I don't know, sheriff," the tracker questioned, "but they're headed in the same direction as your six riders and it looks like they came from Benton Springs."

"Maybe two more robbers?" the deputy suggested

"Nah, there wouldn't be a reason for them to be split up.

They would all be together," Sheriff Peck answered as he pondered the possibilities.

"You're right. All of the robbers would be here at the same time," the deputy noted. "So who are these two?"

"Someone meeting up with them, maybe?" the sheriff said as he pondered this news which was becoming just as baffling as the other facts.

"Sheriff, there's something else." The tracker said as he walked over to the front of the stagecoach and pointed over to the far side of the road. "There's a set of tracks coming from over there next to where the grave is and heading off in the same direction as all the others."

"I would say it could be some of the passengers," the sheriff suggested, "but that just puts us back assuming the passengers buried the body."

"It can't be the passengers," the tracker corrected him. "That would be too many horses."

"Alright then who do *they* belong to?"

"I'm not sure but it was whoever dug the grave."

"Did the gravediggers leave last?"

"No, the ones coming from Benton Springs left last."

"How can you tell?"

"The dust hasn't erased as much of their tracks as it has the others."

The comment peaked the sheriff's attention. "How long ago are we talking for the last pair of tracks?"

"A couple of hours, but no more than that."

"So, now we have four groups riding off in the same direction," Sheriff Peck pointed out curiously, rubbing the sweat from the back of his neck. "What is going on here?"

"What do we do now, sheriff?" the deputy asked. "Are we going after them?"

"Not with just the three of us. There's at least well over a dozen people out there, all headed in the same direction. We don't know how many are the bad guys and how many are the good guys, if there even are some that are good. We wouldn't know who we were after or what to expect when we found them. For now, we have to assume that the passengers took the payroll or else why would the other three sets of riders be after them?"

"Maybe the passengers took the money and the rest of the robbers came here after the passengers left, found their friends here dead and went off after them."

"That makes sense except for one thing: who buried *this* guy?"

The deputy wanted to respond, but he didn't have a good enough answer to do so. While he was taking in all of the details, the tracker spoke up. "Could the larger group of riders be a posse?"

"No," Sheriff Peck explained. "They would had to have come from Benton Springs. The sheriff there is who notified me that the stage hadn't arrived so he didn't know anything about this."

"Then, do we go back to Jackson Creek and get our own posse?"

"I couldn't get enough men together to go up against that many men," Sheriff Peck insisted, a thin grain of worry in his voice. "Besides, there's no time. By the time we got back to town, got a posse together and made it back here they'd be long gone, assuming we could even find that many men who could come. I'll have to telegraph the sheriff in Hurley and let him know that he's going to be getting some visitors."

# CHAPTER ELEVEN

Billy Richmond sat at the post he had chosen, gazing out at the valley just below him, his perch some seventy feet above it and neatly nestled in the edge of the forest. His position gave him a wide look at anything that could be behind him, giving him ample time to warn the others to prepare for followers of any kind. Even so, the blackness of the night covered the valley like a blanket, doing well to help conceal their camp, but also making it that much harder to spot approaching horses. There was a faint breeze stirring, the smell of ponderosa pine and spruce fir with hints of lavender caressing the air. The countless stars dotting the skies were an amazing spectacle, but did little to compensate for the lack of a fuller moon that could work to their advantage by casting shadows. Off in the distance the howling of a wolf was answered by another who seemed to be equally alone and behind him he periodically heard the calling of an owl announcing his presence while it searched the nighttime for an appropriate meal.

Since the sun had disappeared the breeze coming off of the side of the mountain was chilling, the bursts of colder air causing him to raise his collar and cinch it tightly around his neck in a feeble attempt to ward off its effect. He cupped his hands tightly together, sharing the heated air from his lungs into them in an attempt to warm them.

He was looking forward to the fact that his relief would be there soon, allowing him his opportunity to dine on whatever he had been forced to smell cooking over the past few hours. His stomach had alerted him of the cooking early on, but he was still forced to suffer through its aroma as it wafted through the forest and over to him.

Billy huddled tightly in a knot compressing his body upon itself in an attempt to conserve body heat. A fire would feel so nice right now, he thought, but he dared not commit such a discretion and give away their location since everyone was counting on him to keep them safe.

His preoccupied thoughts were interrupted by the sound of rustling from the bushes behind him. He could hear the faint sound of small twigs crunching under approaching footsteps that were just quiet enough to startle him until he could see who it was. He instantly drew his revolver and waited.

"Billy," a low voice called out softly. "It's Cord."

"It's okay, Cord," Billy responded with a sound of relief, both from hearing a friendly voice again and for the satisfaction that he would soon be dining by a warm fire. He holstered his gun and waited for Cord to appear.

Cord surfaced from the bushes with his rifle in his left hand while holding the collar of his coat together with his right. He meandered over to Billy who was none too eager to head back to camp.

"It's a bit nippy up here," Cord pointed out as he reached Billy's perch and tugged at his coat. "I'd forgotten just how much cooler the nights are up here. I took a gamble that I was even going to need this."

"Yeah, the temperature has dropped quite a bit since the sun went down."

"No kidding," Cord reiterated. "Have you seen any movement down there?"

"Nothing. It's been quiet."

"Good. That's what we want. Go get you some dinner while the food is still warm."

"You don't have to tell me twice," Billy spoke as he had already began to savored the taste of the venison steak early on. He grabbed his rifle and headed back in the direction Cord had just traveled, eager to get to the fire and the food.

Cord watched Billy disappear back into the forest canopy before taking his uncomfortable seat on the plateau overlooking the valley. He had gone over the timeline and he didn't anticipate Frank Quincey coming into view anytime soon, but, then again, he didn't know how pressing Quincey would be on his horses. Still, the man would have to come down the valley he was staring at unless he wanted to take a longer route and be concealed by the cover of the trees. Knowing what he did about the type of person Quincey was he couldn't imagine him taking the harder path. He wouldn't want to waste the time nor was he concerned about being discreet. He was man on a mission.

The next several hours seemed to drag by, the wind stirring more with bursts of colder air slamming into him as he sat exposed on the rock ledge. He could expect Nathan to relieve him in another hour or so, giving him just a few brief hours of slumber before having to wake and head out again under the cover of night.

The pace was exhausting, but necessary if they were to stand a chance of staying a comfortable distance ahead of Quincey. By his calculation, they were still almost two full days from Hurley. If they had to, they would skip camping the final night and push through to town without stopping, provided the horses continued to hold up.

Cord hated the thought of River Holloway sleeping peacefully as the rest of them took turns sitting out here shivering in the cold to keep the others safe but he didn't trust the man enough that he would fulfill his part of their obligation. All it would take was one careless watch and Quincey and his men would be upon them with no way to defend themselves. It simply wasn't worth the risk they would be taking.

He knew the rise to get a start on the trail was going to be early, but he expected no less of their pursuers. They had to stay one step ahead of them if they were to have any chance at all of making it to Hurley in time. He had heard of the sheriff there, Sage Connelly, and knew he was someone who could be counted on for protection.

Connelly had made a name for himself over the years as a peacekeeper of the highest caliber, unrelenting in keeping the law and unwilling to ever back down. He was tenacious in preserving the peace and would just as soon take a bullet than to discredit the badge he wore. Cord hated the thought of bringing such a fight to Connelly's town but the truth of the matter was he was the only one who had a chance of helping them make it through this alive. And right now, they needed every chance they could get their hands on.

An hour passed as he sat, trembling with a chill passing over him. Despite his best efforts, the cold was seeping through his layers of clothing when Nathan Brooks appeared from the woods behind him.

"Hey," the man spoke softly.

"Hey."

"Ready for some relief?"

"Sure, if you're ready to freeze a little."

"No, but I don't really have a choice."

"Sorry."

"Just do me a favor, will 'ya?" Nathan asked as he took the spot on the rock ledge, "Have some coffee going when I come back."

"Will do," Cord assured him. "I'm not going back to sleep so there'll be plenty brewed when you come in." Nathan threw him a silent wave as Cord gathered his rifle and nodded before heading back towards camp.

The walk back wasn't a far distance, but the anticipation of warm coffee filling his chilled body made the journey seem exponentially farther. When he arrived back at camp everyone was fast asleep and the fire was just short of nonexistent. He generously piled small branches onto it, quickly reviving its survival as he anxiously hovered his chilled hands over it, feeling its warmth cascade over the front of his body as he tried to ignore his icy back. He glanced over at River and Holbrook, both of whom were oblivious to what was happening, both sleeping peacefully in their warm beddings. It was just as well. Neither of them would be of any use in a fight, either one of a physical nature or one using guns. The best they could hope for if fighting broke out was to arm the men and have them fire in a specific direction in the hopes of at least hitting something. Cord also questioned if River would even be willing to put up a fight. He feared the man would sit idly by, waiting for the opportunity for Cord and Nathan to become injured or killed, allowing him, River, to abscond with the payroll money. He was just the type of person to do it. Cord had just fed the fire another handful of wood when he heard Madeline begin to stir behind him.

"Sorry," he apologized quietly. "Didn't mean to wake you."

"It's fine," she said as she sat up and tried clumsily to gather herself and fix her hair. "I wasn't sleeping very sound, anyway." She positioned herself closer to the fire, extending her hands in front of it to take in its warmth. "What time is it?"

"A little after four. I was going to wake everyone here soon and get started breaking down the camp so we can get a head start. We need to cover as much ground today as possible."

"Is there anything I can do to help?"

"That depends. Can you cook?"

"Of course, I can cook. Are you being sarcastic asking me that because I'm a woman?"

"No, I'm asking you that because we're going to be hungry."

"Oh," she responded, feeling a little embarrassed for being defensive. "Yes, I can cook."

"If you wouldn't mind," he said carefully, "could you make breakfast while I saddle all the horses and start getting our bedrolls put up?"

"Sure. Sorry about that," she said apologetically.

After sufficiently fueling the campfire, Cord walked over and lightly kicked Holbrook and River awake, taking great care not to disturb Billy. Both men threw Cord a dissatisfied glance as they rustled out of their comfort and into the chilly early hour while Madeline had already begun to work on making breakfast.

The activity around camp progressed on through breakfast and into everyone packing their things up and preparing to leave. Nathan had returned just in time to choke down his breakfast and plenty of hot coffee quickly before they all stepped into their saddles and headed out down the hills and onto the valley, uneasy and unsure of what the day held for them.


Pacing back and forth wasn't doing anything to calm Frank Quincey's already fragile nerves. He had been on edge all day and night since finding out his baby brother, Virgil, had been killed. But that was only part to his aggravation. Not only was his brother dead, but he knew where the people responsible were and he could do nothing about it until the indian tracker caught up with them.

His men knew better than to question his motives concerning jobs, but no one cared to bring up his loss. Quincey had a violent temper, the type that could never be reasoned with, the type that no one was safe around. It was better to give him his space and let his rage come out on those that he hunted.

Fox had tried talking to Quincey off and on while they waited but it did not matter. The man was obsessed and could not be distracted. He had hatred in his eyes, the kind that wouldn't be satisfied with just killing these people, but preferred to watch them suffer in the process. A bullet was too good for them, he would say, they deserved to feel the anguish of seeing their lives slowly being taken from them. They needed to feel the pain as he felt it. Then, he would gladly put them out of their misery.

When darkness was cast over the valley, Quincey's demeanor took a turn for the worst. He erupted during supper, throwing things about and cursing wildly, set off by the tiniest of details his eyes overwhelmed with hatred. His patience had disappeared long ago and his men were now nervous to even be around him for fear that one thing would set him off. Their fears were justified since it wasn't beyond him to shoot one of his own men who had caused him grief. They gave him his space and watched the trail behind them, wishing the rest of the crew would arrive before Quincey lost it and snapped.

"Where the hell are they?!" Quincey demanded as he began pacing about, his features cold and stiff. "They should have been here by now!"

One man attempted to reassure him. "Lee had to get them from the herd…"

"I know he had to get them from the herd!" Quincey cut him off short. But where the hell was the herd? Texas?! They've taken so long that now we've lost daylight. Now we'll have to wait until morning to get a start."

"At least it'll give the horses time to get in a good rest," one of the men offered.

Quincey turned and glared at the man, his eyes casting a hateful look at him. "Is that supposed to make me feel better?" he asked sarcastically. "Do you think I give a damn about those horses?! I don't care if we have to walk to Hurley, I'm not letting these people go! Get that through your thick skull!"

Thoroughly enraged, Quincey turned to walk away from his men when he heard a single horse approaching from the valley in front of them. He stood his ground as the rider came into view. When he was close enough the men could see that it was Fox.

"Where's he coming from?" one of the men asked to the group.

Quincey answered with his back to them as he watched Fox ride up. "I sent him up ahead to see if he could spot a fire or anything else that would tell us if we're heading in the right direction," he said as Fox pulled up and climbed down. "Well?" Quincey asked with a hint of hope in his voice.

"I'm sorry, Frank, but I didn't see anything," Fox admitted hesitantly, as he stepped over to their fire and poured a cup of coffee. He tried to take a stinging sip, frowning from the burn to his mouth before he continued. "I went a couple of miles up so if they were following the valley they're at least a half a day ahead of us. If they took the shortcut across the hills it could be even more than that."

The news did not settle well with Quincey. He could feel

his gain on those he followed slipping farther and farther away from him, his revenge slipping through his fingers. They had a little less than two days to catch up with them or they will have made it to Hurley and with Sage Connelly as sheriff they would be safe there, and that was with forgetting about the money, the very same tainted money that had cost Virgil his life. He didn't want to think about it since it would seem as if he was putting a price on his brother's life, but when he finished with the people responsible, the money would be the icing on the cake. He owed Virgil that much.

# CHAPTER TWELVE



It was a crisp, clear morning as Frank Quincey eyed the man with aggravation as he stared down at him. Fox was kneeling down onto the ground, carefully looking for signs of a trail that had appeared to have vanished from right in front of their eyes. Fox walked the small area over and over, retracing the same steps and trying to pick up on new tracks laid by Cord and the others, but had been unsuccessful as of yet.

"What's the matter?" Quincey inquired. "Can't you find it?"

"No," Fox admitted reluctantly. "It's like I said, Frank, I can only track them so far before we lose them. Looks like they've peeled off into the hills for cover trying to throw us off."

"You don't see anything? Nothing?"

"I'm sorry, Frank, but I'm afraid I'm just not good enough to track them over rock. You're going to have to sit tight and wait for the indian to get here."

The news had been a long time coming, but even so it still wasn't what Quincey had wanted to hear. Now, all that hard riding to try to catch up to them had been put on hold while they sat on their hands and waited. Waited for who knew how long. Waited while Virgil's murderers got further and further away from them. The thought sickened him.

"Can't we just stay on this trail and keep going towards Hurley?"

"We could, but it's the long way around," Fox informed him. "They're cutting through the hills to cut off time. If you don't stay on their heels you're taking the chance that they might change their minds and head elsewhere. We'd take the chance of losing them somewhere between here and there."

"But the next closest town is Hurley," Quincey pointed out.

"Yeah, but what if they decided to go elsewhere? They already know that we're after them so they know we think they're going to Hurley. But what if they don't? Maybe they decide to throw us a curve and head over to Marsville. It's further away, but we'd never know they had changed their minds until we had made it all the way to Hurley and found out that they weren't even there. By then it'd be too late to catch up with them."

Quincey agreed with the logic, though he didn't much care for it in the least, especially since it had such a strong possibility of being true. He didn't like the idea of being forced to follow them, but it was the only way to be sure where they were going to end up. The thought of having to wait for the indian to catch up to them was troubling enough, but even more troubling was the mere thought that they could lose them altogether.

"This is just great," Frank spouted angrily as he repositioned himself in his saddle. "We get to sit by and cool our heels while they keep getting farther and farther away from us."

"I'm sorry, Frank," Fox offered an apology, but Quincey was too wound up to acknowledge it. He jerked the reins of his horse and walked it over to the nearest tree before swinging down and tying it off.

"You might as well get down and take a seat," he said reluctantly to his men. "Looks like we're gonna be sitting here awhile."


It was still dark when the line of horses carrying Cord and the others wound through the trees, edging the hillsides and weaving along as they meticulously followed a faint game trail. The going was not considerably slower than following the usual trail out in the open, but it was still enough for Cord to receive questionable looks from both Holbrook and River.

Cord's last concern were what the two men thought of him or his decisions. Neither or them interested Cord. All he knew was that they had to make it to Hurley however they could. There was no time for discussions or opinions. None of that mattered. He would do what he had to in order to get them there safely.

They had made up quite a bit of ground when the first shards of sunlight began spilling over the horizon of the hills. Cord welcomed its presence not only to allow them to speed up their pace but also the warmth it brought helped to bring him out of his exhausted, groggy state of mind. As the heat began radiating over the valley and splashing off the hillsides, Cord happily removed his coat and tucked it into his bedroll as his muscles began soaking in the warmth.

He glanced back at the others, making sure that everyone was keeping up. Madeline was directly behind him and, as was her nature, had not uttered a word of complaint. Behind her was Billy Richmond followed by Holbrook, Tell and then River. Nathan brought up the rear of the group, his place-ment a result of the discussion he had had with Cord to make certain the group stayed together. It was also Cord's way of conveniently keeping an eye on River, a task that he felt was more important now than ever, especially since they were getting closer to Hurley. He did not trust the man not to try to take off with at least some of the payroll money that he had remained so interested in since the stagecoach. He had been listening in on Cord's directions about the location of Hurley that he would easily be able to navigate his way there from their current position. The reality was the closer they got to town, the more of a threat River posed to them.

"Can't we just stop for awhile and eat something?" Holbrook said, breaking the silence of the chilled morning. Cord knew the comment was directed at him, though he didn't feel like explaining it to them all over again since he had informed everyone the night before of their plans. Still, he felt he had to since he knew the man wasn't going to let the issue go.

"We've already discussed this, Holbrook. We have to keep moving as much as we can to stay ahead of Quincey."

"I don't seem to recall the vote that elected you as spokesperson for all of us," River chimed in, his drawl making the comment that much more irritating for Cord to hear.

"You're welcome to stay behind and have a leisurely breakfast, if you'd like, River," Cord responded dryly. "Just give Quincey our apologies for not joining you."

"You act as if I have something to fear," River said cooly. "I, myself, have not wronged the man, therefore, I have no reason to be afraid of him or his wrath. You, on the other hand, were the gentleman that killed his kin, not I."

"Yeah, but Quincey doesn't know that," Cord pointed out. "He only knows that his brother was killed. He doesn't know who pulled the trigger, nor does he care."

"Then I shall inform him that it was not I who took the

man's life. Surely he can see that I am not one who carries a gun."

"You're not understanding. Frank Quincey doesn't care if you carry a gun or not. All he cares about is killing each and every one of us to make sure he gets the right person."

"Then I shall appeal to his common sense. Perhaps if we offer him the money he will have mercy on those of us that had nothing to do with it."

Cord shook his head. "So you want to offer him money for his brother's life, huh? No, that won't make him mad, at all. I've got news for you, he'd kill you just for suggesting it. Men like Quincey can't be bargained with and they certainly can't be bought. No amount of money is going to change his mind and he won't stop until he sees all of us dead."

"Can we at least try to give him the money?" Holbrook broke in. "We won't know for sure until we try."

"I'm telling you it won't make a difference," Cord tried to impress on him. "We're turning the money in to the sheriff and the bank. No one's going to use it to try to ransom our lives."

The conversation died off as they continued filing through the hills with Cord periodically stopping and glancing back behind them. He didn't expect to see anyone this soon, but, then again, he wasn't convinced that Quincey wasn't riding his horses into the ground.

The morning passed without incident or further discussion about handing over the money. Cord knew River was plotting something. He had let the thought of paying off Quincey go too easily. That could only mean one thing. He was plotting to take the money himself. If he felt they were all doomed anyway, why not take the money and remove himself from the danger? That way, he would be alive and rich. Such an idea was not beyond River's capabilities and knowing this caused Cord to be on high alert at the man's movements.

It was around midday when they came upon an outcropping of boulders at the base of one of the hills. Cord felt it was a good spot to let the horses take a breather and stopped his horse, turning it to face the others.

"Why are we stopping?" Madeline asked.

"We're giving the horses a break," he explained as he swung down from the Shire. "You look like you could use one, too," he added.

"Thanks, I guess, although I'm not really sure how to take that," she responded as she climbed down from her own stead. "But to be honest, I could use a few minutes to stretch my legs."

"Well, take advantage of it because we're not staying put too long. We've got to get back out there and keep moving."

Everyone dismounted and milled about, trying to shake off their exhaustion. They had been pushing themselves past their comfort level not to mention how the ride was beginning to take its toll on all of them, including Cord, but he dared not wait too long to get back at it. He continued glancing over his shoulder expecting at any moment to see Quincey and his team of men bounding over the hill charging full speed after them. He just hoped that time was still a ways off. He was still considering their situation when Nathan walked over to him. "What d'ya think?"

Cord leaned closer so the others couldn't hear the concern in his voice. "I didn't want to alarm anyone, but I'm starting to get concerned about how much ground we're covering."

"You think we need to go faster?" Nathan asked.

"That's just it. I don't think we can. We're already pushing the horses pretty hard. We can't afford to lose them or we'll really be in a bad spot."

"Do you think we need to make a stand and fight it out?"

"No, we'd end up on the losing end of that. Quincey could surround us and wait it out. We'd have nowhere to go."

"Well, we can't lighten the load anymore than we already have. They left most of their things back at the stagecoach."

"I know," Cord agreed, but it didn't help him feel any better about the situation. "I don't know what else to do. I keep imagining Quincey coming over the hill right behind us. I guess all we can do is to keep moving and hope for the best."

He started to say something else until he realized River had walked up behind them and was within hearing distance to pick up on their conversation. Both Cord and Nathan stood quietly, not knowing what to say in the moment. River didn't speak, but walked casually past them and over to where Holbrook was sitting on a boulder wiping the perspiration from his face with a handkerchief. River settled into a seat next to him and began talking to him. Cord knew he had probably overheard enough to pass it on to Holbrook. A few minutes later, River walked back over to his horse as Holbrook walked over to join Cord who was scouting out the land directly before them.

"Cord, I think we need to talk about the payroll money," Holbrook insisted.

"Payroll?" Cord heard someone say behind him. He swung his head around and saw Tell standing a few feet away. He had not realized that the young man had been approaching him when Holbrook mentioned the money. "What payroll?"

Cord tried his best to dismiss the subject. "It's nothing."

Holbrook turned to address the young man. "We picked up the payroll that the stage was carrying when it was robbed."

"*Robbed?*" Tell asked curiously as he looked to Cord for an explanation.

Cord's mouth tightened as he tried to hide his irritation as he reluctantly answered his query. "Some men tried to rob the stage we were on. The driver and the foreman were killed. We brought the money with us to turn in."

"How much are we talking about?" Tell wondered.

Before Cord could open his mouth to dismiss his question, Holbrook spilled the answer. "Twenty-seven thousand dollars."

"Really? Wow!" Tell exclaimed with a shocked expression. "No wonder you're in such a hurry to get to Hurley!"

"We tried to get Cord to leave the money for Frank Quincey, but he won't do it."

"Who's Frank Quincey?"

"He's the man who's following us."

"Wait...someone's following us? Who's following us?"

"Frank Quincey," Holbrook repeated. "Cord shot his brother during the robbery."

Tell glanced from Holbrook over to Cord, his mouth still hanging open in amazement at the news. He was about to ask Cord something but Cord was too frustrated and walked away, silently cursing under his breath at what Holbrook had done. All he needed was to have another person to have to watch over about the money, especially since he knew nothing about the young man. He cast a disgusted glance at Madeline as he passed her, not intending for it to be directed at her, but to show that he was not in the mood to take the time to explain what had just happened. All he wanted to do now was to get started again on the trail. He grabbed the reins of the Shire and began walking it away as he tried to dismiss this new bad luck.

Things were getting out of hand.

# CHAPTER THIRTEEN

Frank Quincey was staring off in the direction they had just traveled, kicking hand-size rocks about and throwing away pieces of the small branch he had frustratingly been tearing apart while he waited. The three men with him were all lounging under a small collection of trees, two of whom had dozed off while the third was lazily whittling away at a small piece of fallen pine he had discovered.

Quincey was not a patient man, not by far, and did not do well whenever he could not control the circumstances around him. He was accustomed to being in charge and being able to dictate his own path, but this time that been taken away from him and he was not taking it very well. His absence of patience was bleeding through the longer he had to wait.

"Where the hell are they?" he snapped at Fox, who had been sitting idly under a tree just a few feet away.

"I don't know, Frank. I would think they would be along any time now. It depends on how long it takes them to bring the herd in and get them to the stockyards."

Quincey mulled over the answer, already aware of the

reasoning behind the delay, but still needing to hear it from someone else. He knew the setup of the stockyards but it did not ease his impatience. His men were loyal to him, that he never questioned, but the waiting was ripping him apart. He needed to get this handled, now. If his men saw this action go unpunished it would undermine his very authority and that he could not have. His reputation was what kept him in business and what worked to keep the law from coming after him more aggressively. He knew that eventually a lawman would come along that wasn't intimidated by him or his past and they would be responsible for his decline and his ultimate demise. So far, that lawman had not come forward, but he knew they were out there, somewhere. Until then, he would continue on with his operation and conduct business as usual. When that someone finally came along and developed enough of a backbone to kill him, then they would do so.

"Frank!" came the call from the man who had been whittling. The call brought Frank's attention around to the thundering of horse's hooves that was faintly coming up from behind him. When Frank fixed his eyes far enough away he saw what he had been anxiously waiting for. The remainder of his men topped the last hill and came into view in the valley. It was a welcome sight and one that renewed his hope that they would finally be able to catch up with the passengers before they made it to Hurley.

"Let's go, boys!" Frank commanded as the two sleeping men scrambled from their slumber and mounted their horses with Frank and Fox. They sat in their saddles and waited for the group to ascend upon them, fourteen of his men plus the indian tracker, Red Bear. They rode up to Quincey and the others, eager to hear what he had to say to them.

"Thought we'd never get here," the leader of the group announced as he pulled his horse to a stop. "We didn't realize how far out you were."

"What took you so long?" Quincey asked with a generous bit of irritation in his voice, although already knowing the answer.

"Sorry, Frank, but we had to wait until we could get the cattle brought in. We got here as fast as we could. Lee filled us in what what was happening."

"I want these people caught," Quincey announced to them without hesitation. "I want them caught and I want them dead. You hear? I want every one of them dead. They don't get away with this. Do you hear me? None of them."

"Lee told us they robbed a stagecoach," one of the men asked."Is that true?"

"I don't know anything about the money, if that's what you're asking" Quincey admitted to them. "Virgil took it upon himself to plan a stagecoach robbery without my knowledge. That's what got him killed and that's why we're going after them. The money is the least of my concerns." Quincey drew his horse over to Red Bear's horse and locked eyes with the man. "They've gone off the trail," he informed the indian bluntly. "I need you to find their trail and track 'em down. There should be six of them."

Red Bear nodded without expression, his hard, cold eyes almost slicing through Quincey's. The indian was hard and distant and even though Frank Quincey had employed him several times before he still knew that the indian had no love for the white man, not any white man, including him. Though Red Bear's hatred for the white man was no secret, his hatred for those that Frank Quincey sought was much greater and that was the edge that Quincey would use to his advantage. He knew the indian would not stop short of finding them no matter how long it took or how far they had to go. He had never let him down before and Quincey knew he wouldn't start now.

Red Bear climbed down from his pinto and carefully

studied the tracks where they left the trail and appeared to disappear into the hills. Fox began to dismount but Quincey held up his hand to stop him.

"I was just going to show him the last place where I think they went." Fox explained.

"He doesn't need your help," Quincey cited without taking his eyes off of the indian. "Don't worry. He's got it."

Red Bear studied the spot for mere seconds and glanced over to Quincey while motioning off in the direction they needed to go. "That wasn't the way I thought they went," Fox admitted sheepishly.

Quincey stared at Fox with a look of satisfaction. "That's why *he's* here."


The telegraph sprang to life, clicking away its content to the man in the telegraph office. The operator had been standing outside the window of the telegraph office talking to one of the townspeople about the arrival of the afternoon train when he heard the familiar clicking of an incoming message. He scurried around the corner and sat down at his desk, scribbling out the content with the pencil he had tucked behind his ear as it repeated itself and checking it twice to ensure its validity. It was then that he realized what it entailed, causing him to tear the paper from his note pad and hurry out the door and over to the sheriff's office, anxiously grasping the note with a sweaty hand. He made the distance to the sheriff in quick time, entering the door just as the sheriff was seating himself at his desk. The sudden appearance of the clerk in his office caused the man to stop searching for the papers he had on his mind and focus on what was being delivered to him.

"Got an urgent message for you, sheriff," the nervous

slender man with a bushy mustache and wire rimmed glasses announced as he handed the paper over to the sheriff. The man wearing the badge glanced at the operator as he quietly took the folded paper from his hand and opened it. He quickly scanned its contents and looked off to nothing as he briefly pondered its message.

"What'cha gonna do, sheriff?" the nervous operator asked with concern. "Is there gonna be trouble?"

Sheriff Sage Connelly looked over at the man who was anxiously awaiting news. He hesitated to offer any information to the man, knowing that by doing so it would cause the town's rumor mill to go into high gear at the hint of such news and the last thing he needed was to set a panic into motion. He had experienced such a panic before and did not wish to repeat the tragedy. Instead, he decided to take the conversation in another, safer direction. "Did you tell anyone else about this?" Sheriff Connelly asked with a concerned expression as he held up the note for the clerk to see.

"No, sheriff," the man assured him with a nervous shaking of his head. "I came straight here."

"Good. I want to keep it that way," he said solemnly. "I don't want you breathing a word of this to anyone, not anyone. Understand?"

"Sure thing, sheriff," the clerk agreed.

Sheriff Connelly waved the note in the air in front of him for the man to see as his way of thanking him, causing the clerk to nod and turn as he hurried back out the door and back to the telegraph office. But Connelly was no fool. Despite his warnings, he knew the clerk would only be able to contain himself for so long before he could no longer stand it and would have to tell someone of the news. But at least it would buy him some time, albeit not very much. Word would spread through Hurley like a raging wildfire and the townspeople would be swept up in it and consumed with it just as quickly. Once word got out there would be no stopping its progression and then panic would inevitably ensue. By then, there would no need to assign blame on how it got started. That would be a waste of time and effort. The point was to keep everyone as calm as possible, for as long as possible.

Connelly was a hard man who lived by strict standards. For those who didn't know him he came across as blunt, but fair. Those in town knew him to be honest and reliable. Those who did not know him soon learned that he was also a man who did not back down and was not to be reckoned with.

He had not always been a lawman. There was a time that he was a cowhand, herding cattle and drifting from job to job trying to find his niche in the territory. But a chance encounter with a rancher with a questionable past in Hurley crossed paths with Connelly and tried to have him removed. The rancher soon discovered just how dangerous Connelly could be when provoked. The rancher killed the town's sheriff, but when he tried to get rid of Connelly, he came up short. And dead. Connelly was offered the job of sheriff and had been there ever since.

Sheriff Sage Connelly folded the note and tucked it into his shirt pocket as he walked out his office door and stopped on the boardwalk, glancing in all directions in search of his deputy, Tom Wills. Wills had been by his side for a little more than four years now and had been the most devoted and reliable man he had ever had the pleasure of working with since first pinning on a badge.

He knew he could count on the man's discretion and right now, he needed it more than ever to quell the situation that was about to unfold on them. Sheriff Connelly started up the street heading for the main cluster of businesses that would be the most likely to produce Deputy Wills' appearance. He had made it to the fourth business when he located Deputy Tom Wills. Wills was talking to several men in the barber shop when Sheriff Connelly walked in and interrupted their discussion.

"Hey, sheriff, how are things?" a burly Swede named Gustafson asked causally as he continued clipped away at a customer's hair.

"Morning, Gus. Morning, Herb," Sheriff Connelly said addressing both men at once.

"Morning, sheriff," the man called Herb said as he returned the gesture with a smile.

"What can we do for you, sheriff?" Gustafson asked with his usual grin without looking up from his work.

"I'm afraid I need to borrow Tom here for a few minutes," Sheriff Connelly casually answered.

"That's okay, sheriff," Gustafson's booming voice conceded. "We weren't believing his story about shooting those grouse, anyway, were we Herb?"

"No, we weren't," Herb replied with a playful grin. "I think it took him a few more shots than he's letting on."

"Well, you boys know how Tom always likes to embellish the truth a little when he's talking about his hunting skills," Sheriff Connelly said with a faint grin. The comment aroused a roar of laughter from the men as they pointed an accusatory finger at the deputy as if he had been caught in a lie. While the men enjoyed their humor at the deputy's expense Sheriff Connelly made eye contact with Deputy Tom Wills and nodded his head in the direction of outside. "See you fellas later," he announced to the men, who were still finding humor in the deputy's embarrassment. The men tossed a cheerful wave at the sheriff and Tom as the two walked outside. When they had shut the door and walked a few steps away from the door and over on the boardwalk, Sheriff Connelly turned to his deputy.

"What's up, sheriff?" the man asked curiously.

"We've got a situation," he started while making sure to keep his voice down. "I just got a telegraph from Sheriff Peck in Jackson Creek. Their stage was robbed between there and Benton Springs. Both the foreman and the driver were killed. They made off with the payroll and they're headed this way."

# CHAPTER FOURTEEN

With their rest over, Cord and the others started filing out to get back on their way to Hurley. He was furious with Holbrook for sharing the information about the payroll with Tell, who by all accounts was a virtual stranger, potentially putting them in a bad situation. Now, because of his sharing of their secret Cord had to keep an even tighter watch on the money. It was just another job that he didn't need right then. The more he thought about it, the more he needed to make sure Nathan was aware of his concern. He would need his help in guarding the money since it had to be spread out over three horses.

After he started the group heading west, Cord allowed Madeline to pass by him as he dropped back and waited for Nathan who was bringing up the rear of the group. Nathan caught his concerned look and held back until the others had passed far enough ahead so as not to risk being overheard again.

"I think we need to do something with the money," Cord suggested.

"Like what?" Nathan wondered.

"I don't know, but I don't feel right having it sitting out in the open like this hanging over our saddles, especially since we also now have Tell to worry about."

"Do you think he'll try something?"

"I don't know. That's what's so annoying about the situation. We don't know anything about him. For all we know, he could pull his gun on us at anytime, shoot whomever he feels like shooting and then take the money and we would be none the wiser until it was too late to stop him."

"Should we take his gun from him?" Nathan suggested.

"Nah, that would only alert him that we don't trust him. That might be just the thing to coax him into trying something. Besides, he would need it if we get surprised and have to shoot it out with Quincey and his gang."

"Well, if he's going to try something it's going to happen regardless of whether we initiate it or not."

"I know. That's the problem. Do we make the first move or take the chance and see if he makes a move? Besides, we don't even know if we have anything to worry about."

"I'll play it anyway you want," Nathan reassured him.

"Whatever we do, I think we need to let Madeline and Billy in on it, too."

"You still don't trust River, do you?"

"Nor Holbrook. I can't tell if he mentioned the money to Tell on purpose or if he just wasn't thinking about what he was doing. I don't think he's a threat, but I do think he's a liability that could do something stupid to get us all killed."

"So, what do we do?" Nathan asked.

"I think we quietly put all the money on one horse and not tell anyone."

"Out of sight, out of mind, huh?"

"Yeah. That way, we only have to keep up with one horse and not three. What do you think?"

"Makes sense. Which horse do we use?"

"You and I can't do it because we don't have saddles. Putting aside River, Holbrook and Tell that just leaves Madeline."

"Then let's go with Madeline. Then I can keep a better look on the money from afar. If one of them does try something we'll have an extra gun on them."

"I wanted to suggest that," Cord admitted with an embarrassing grin, "but I didn't want it to sound like I didn't trust you."

"I understand," Nathan responded with his own grin. "I would have felt the same way if the roles had been reversed."

"Good. So we're on the same page here?"

"Yeah. But how do we make the transfer without someone else seeing us?"

"We'll do it tonight when we stop for the night, right in the middle of the camp being set up when everyone's attention is diverted."

"Got it," Nathan nodded. Cord acknowledged the same and rode away back up to the lead, feeling a little better about their situation.

The group made good time for the remainder of the day, only stopping once more before deciding to stop and settling into a camp next to an overhang. The spot was partially concealed from the valley below and yet cut back into the rock walls to offer some overhead protection from the elements. The location was several hundred feet above the valley floor and gave them a clear view of anyone who would be coming from behind them for quite a distance. A flat grassy area off to the left of it was ideal for tying off the horses while still keeping them close enough to allow for a fast getaway, should they need it.

Cord had made it a point to distance himself from River throughout the day, feeling it was better than possibly getting into another confrontation with the man. Holbrook had remained relatively quiet and Tell had only engaged in casual conversation with he and Madeline.

As they began to set up their camp, Cord motioned to Nathan until he got his attention and motioned for him to come over to where he was setting up his bedding. Nathan casually walked over bringing the bag of money he had been in charge of with him while River, Holbrook and Tell were busy taking care of the horses. Cord walked over to Madeline and whispered in her ear what they were planning. When she nodded in agreement, Cord took the bag of money he had been carrying strapped to the Shire and placed it under Madeline's overturned saddle along with Nathan's bag of money. They managed to get them covered before any of the three men were able to make it back to camp.

A relieved Cord felt better about having the money all together and focused on what lay ahead of them tomorrow. He looked forward to being done with their excursion. If everything went well they would be in Hurley by late tomorrow and his worrying about the money, and their safety, would finally be over. Of course, it would mean getting another early start in the morning and pushing the horses all day, but it was still possible, unless they ran into trouble. And the way this trip had progressed, it was obvious that anything was possible.

The group settled down for the night knowing it would be another short one, but at least the last one. Tomorrow they would be safely in Hurley where they could seek out the protection of the law and the townspeople. In order to make that happen they needed to be on the trail long before daylight if they were to stay far enough ahead of their pursuers to stay safe and to have any sort of a chance of making it there in time. The one thing they had going for them was that there had still been no sign of Quincey and his men, a good sign but one that still filled them with concern.

No one had voiced such of a concern although secretly it filled the minds of most every one of them, expect for River, Cord decided. The last thing they needed was to see Quincey and his men topping the hills bearing down on them giving them little to no warning. Cord would have preferred to see them coming at them from far off in the distance instead of being surprised. At least that way he would know *when* he was coming.

Cord wandered around camp as everyone was settling down for the night. They had chosen to keep only as large of a fire as necessary for warmth that evening and nothing more. The less they could be spotted from the valley the better. Cord had tried to keep off the main game trails as much as possible and stay in the hills where it proved to be better cover. It was slower going than crossing the valley, but still a necessary measure for them to hide their tracks as much as possible. Cord wasn't an excellent tracker but he did have enough experience following tracks to lay down what he hoped to be a sufficient faint trail. He knew the average man would have difficulty following them. With the way he was routing their movements it would take an experienced tracker to stay on their heels.

He checked on each person in the camp as he made his rounds to make sure everyone was keeping as low of a profile as they could. Billy was bedded down next to Madeline engaging her in conversation, as usual. Holbrook was sitting by the fire going through the contents of his satchel, for whatever reason Cord couldn't imagine. Tell was talking with River who saw Cord walking up and gave him an insincere nod as he eyed him carefully until he had passed them while Nathan was absent, having agreed to take the first watch. For the most part everyone seemed to be in relatively good spirits, considering the circumstances, which was a relief for Cord and gave him the best peace of mind as he had had since they had departed from the stagecoach. Still, he was looking forward to this being his last night camping out in the hills.

When he had circled his way back to the camp, he found himself wanting to spend some time with Madeline. He had been so preoccupied with keeping everyone moving and keeping track of the money that he had neglected being able to spend time with her and to get to know her better.

Madeline was a striking woman with dark brown hair and matching eyes. She had a confidence about her, such as from a woman who knew what she wanted and wasn't afraid to put forth the effort to get it, but not so much so that she could be considered as being distant or pretentious. She had packed up her life and come out west to take care of her brother and his growing family which showed she had compassion. She was also fiercely brave, a trait she had exuded throughout their entire ordeal. He could see why a man could fall for her, and fall hard.

It was just before midnight when Cord went out to relieve Nathan from his watch. He glanced down the hills as he approached where he had set up his observation, scanning the area below them for movement or the existence of a fire, but saw nothing. He nodded to the man as he walked up, pulling his coat tighter around his neck as a burst of cold air descended upon them, a disadvantage of being posted in such an exposed area but a necessary one in order to see if someone was on the move.

"Seen anything?" Cord asked nonchalantly as he stepped up beside Nathan.

"Nothing. It's been quiet."

"Well, that's a good thing."

"Yeah, but it's almost too quiet."

"With what we've gone through there's no such thing as too quiet."

Nathan snickered from the comment, knowing that it rang true, now more than ever. "Anything cooking back at camp?"

"Just some beans and hot coffee."

"Forget the beans. Right now, after sitting out here in the cold I'll just take the coffee."

"Good choice."

"I'll send Billy out in a few hours," Nathan said as he grabbed his rifle and stood for Cord to take the seat. "Hopefully, everything will stay quiet."

"Let's hope so," Cord responded with a grin and a faint wave. He watched Nathan disappear into the woods before turning back his attention to the land below them. Between the clouds and only a half-moon his field of vision was somewhat hindered, but there was still a faint enough glow from it and the stars overhead in the sky to offer a small bit of help.

Cord struggled over the next few hours, shifting in his position as much as possible to keep himself warm. Although he didn't invite something to happen the boredom of sitting out here alone along with the stress and exhaustion of being on the move so much these past few days was beginning to take its toll on him. *This was the last night that they had to do this,* he kept telling himself, *and then all of this would finally be over.* He was in a hurry to get rid of the payroll money, too, not wanting the responsibility of keeping up with it any longer than was necessary.

He heard Billy coming up to relieve him long before he saw him. The young man was making quite a bit of noise on his approach, not intentionally, but because of a lack of experience of living out in the wild. Though the nighttime light was scarce Cord could still see his typical grin as he approached where he was sitting.

"Hey, Cord. It sure is a lot colder out here in the open, ain't it?"

"Yeah, but at least this is the last time you'll have to do this," Cord tried optimistically to point out.

"Yeah, that's true," Billy agreed. "So, anything happening out there?"

"Nope. All quiet. Just like we want it."

"Hope it stays that way."

"Well, I'm gone. See you about five," Cord said with a nod as he headed back towards camp. He wanted to catch what little bit of sleep he could fit in before they had to get moving again, but doubted he would be able to do so. A better plan was to sit around the fire trying to warm up with plenty of hot coffee. When he finally made it back to camp, everyone was sound asleep and the fire had all but died out. He added some wood to it, coaxing it back to life. Once it had established itself enough he made more coffee, sitting with his back up against a tree as he savored it. At some point he had dozed off since the next thing he remembered was being shaken awake.

At first, he felt as if he were dreaming, but when he opened his eyes he saw Billy squatting in front of him shaking him by the shoulder. He strained to see out of his groggy eyes as he fought to get his bearings. "What? What is it?"

"Cord. They're coming."

# CHAPTER FIFTEEN

The words instantly startled Cord fully awake.

"Are you sure it's them?"

"Yeah. It was a lot of horses, maybe twenty. I could see the dust being kicked up."

"How far out are they?" he asked as he gathered his rifle and meager belongings and kicked dirt over the glowing embers that was once their camp fire.

"I saw them coming into the valley," Billy informed him as he tried to quell his growing anxiety. "They're still a ways of, but they're coming."

Cord jumped up and reached over to shake Madeline who was tucked soundly in her bedding. "Madeline," he said as he jolted her awake. Her eyes took a second to focus on him as she squinted at his face hanging over her. "Quincey's almost here."

She immediately sprang to her feet and had begun furiously packing up her belongings when Cord grabbed her wrist.

"There's no time for that. Leave it," he instructed her as he released his grip from her arm.

"But we may need these tonight," she insisted as he motioned down at her bedding.

"If Frank Quincey catches up to us, having a bedroll will be the least of our worries." She responded with a quiet nod and grabbed her rifle as Cord and Billy went about the rest of the camp hurriedly waking the others.

"Everybody up," he announced to the others.

"What's going on?" Holbrook asked as he sat up on his elbow while trying to rub the sleep from his eyes.

"Quincey's on his way. Billy just saw him coming up off in the distance heading this way."

"How is that possible?" Tell asked as he stood and started gathering his things. "How can they track you in the dark?"

"I don't know," Cord answered, "but they are."

He walked back over to where Madeline was putting her boots on. "I'm putting all of the payroll bags on your horse so we can keep a better eye on them and I'll put your saddlebag on my horse."

"Alright," she said as she stood and methodically started tying her long hair into a bun. After walking over to Madeline's horse and saddling it he had begun tying the money bags to it when he heard a gun being cocked behind him. The sound caused him to freeze in his tracks.

"I'd be obliged to take those," River announced in his comfortable familiar drawl.

Cord slowly turned to see River standing directly behind him pointing his gun at him. Everyone was scrambling to saddle their horses and stopped to see what was happening. Cord went to reach for his gun but it was then that he realized he had never put it back on from when he had fallen asleep. "Everyone step out away from your horses and your rifles," he instructed them holding the gun on them as they did so. Billy had also not yet put on his gun belt and tried to grab it from where it was lying next to his bedding. River saw the move and fired.

The bullet tore through Billy's upper chest, the force of it knocking him back onto the ground as he called out in intense pain. Madeline screamed.

Cord instinctively started to move to go to check on Billy when River cocked his gun again, forcing Cord to stop. "I need to check on him!" Cord yelled in protest.

"He'll be fine, I assure you," River said calmly. "You just stay right where you are."

Cord looked over at Billy who was lying on his back trying to apply pressure to his wound, but the blood was starting to drip from between his fingers. He wanted desperately to go to the young man, but having just witnessed River's senseless actions he knew he would not be any good to the group if he, too, were shot or worse. "Did it go all the way through?" Cord asked Billy with growing concern as he fought the urge to help him.

"No," Billy answered bluntly as he tightly closed his eyes and cringed from the stabbing pain. Nathan started to go over to help Billy but River moved the gun over to where it also pointed in his direction.

"Everyone stay where you are," River ordered them, "and no one else has to get hurt."

"What are you doing, River?" Cord asked, irritated that the man had chosen this particular time to start something.

"Now, Cord, what does it look like I'm doing? Why, I'm taking the money, of course," River proclaimed proudly.

"Nows not the time for this," Cord insisted. "Not with Quincey right up on us."

"On the contrary, my good man, I would disagree. This is aptly the perfect time. You, sir, are in a hurry to leave. I, on the other hand, want the money. It is grounds for the perfect scenario. Simply hand it over and you can be on your way and

I can be on mine, as well. Stand here and argue with me and I am afraid all you will be doing is delaying your own departure."

"River, it's not our money," Cord tried reasoning with him, though he knew it would do no good. "I made a promise to bring that money back."

"Do not waste your nobility on me, sir, for we both know it is a waste of it. I doubt you have a lily-white background, yourself. Knowing what I do about you and your kind I reason that you have done questionable things in your past, as well, am I correct? Now, I will ask you once more. Please be so kind as to hand over the bags."

Cord stepped around the side of the horse and stood firmly in his place where he could face him. "No."

River did not take the defiance well. He tried his best to hide his impatience, but it was becoming increasingly difficult to do. He was about to speak when Nathan tried to move closer. River kept his eyes on Cord while watching Nathan from the side.

"This does not concern you, Mr. Brooks," River announced to Nathan without looking directly at him. "I would greatly appreciate it if you would be so kind as to stay out of our little disagreement."

"River you're not getting the money," Cord stated flatly.

"Yes, I am and I will do so despite your feeble attempts of heroism to try to stop me," River added. "Mr. Chantry, I must warn you that you are pressing me past my level of patience."

"But it's not your money," Cord repeated through clinched teeth.

"You may keep repeating that, but the reality is that all you are doing is wasting valuable time, time that you desperately need to aid in your escape and to care for young Billy there. You are unnecessarily putting innocent people's lives at stake and for what? A pile of money that is none of your concern nor does it affect your financial standing in any way."

"Don't do this, River," Cord insisted.

"I assure you, sir, as you can see I will shoot you if I must, but I am not leaving here without those bags."

"Cord, we have to go," Nathan interjected. " We've got to get Billy to a doctor. Just give him the bags. Let the law go after him."

A frustrated Cord scoffed out loud and walked back to the horse and began untying the bags. When he had removed the knot he stepped back around holding them. He looked cooly into River's eyes wanting more than anything to kill him, more than he had ever wanted to kill anyone before. As River took a step towards him Cord defiantly dropped the bags onto the ground in front of him. The move angered River, causing him to inhale sharply in agitation, but he wasn't prepared to address it then. He could tell Cord was going to do whatever he could to slow his escape.

"Back up," River instructed Cord with a wave of his gun. Cord took a few steps back holding his hands up for River to see until he was far enough away that River didn't feel threatened by him before turning and calling over to Nathan. "Mr. Brooks, would you be so kind as to tie those onto my horse?"

"Tie 'em on yourself," Nathan replied in protest.

River continued staring at Cord, his gun still pointed at him. "I would ask Mr. Chantry to do it but I feel I need to keep a close eye on him. I assume by the way he handles himself that he has some notable skill with a gun. I would prefer not to give away our location to our pursuers anymore than I already have, but I will not ask you again or I'm afraid I will be forced to kill Mr. Chantry so please secure the bags onto my horse."

Nathan looked over at Cord who nodded slightly. He

watched as Nathan reluctantly picked up the bags and walked them over to River's horse and began tying them on.

"Make sure they are secure, sir," River added as a faint smile formed on his face. "We wouldn't want them to get lost during my departure."

When Nathan was finished, River kept the gun pointed in Cord's direction. "Now, if you would please step away." Nathan continued looking at the man as he backed up enough to satisfy River. As he stepped into the stirrup and threw his leg over the saddle, he continued holding the gun on Cord and Nathan. "You could have saved yourself some valuable time that you are sure to need for your departure if you had simply complied early on. You could come after me if you would like but I suspect you would rather leave out of here while you still can." He pulled the reins of his horse to the side as he spoke. "Despite what you may think of me I do hope that all of you make it to town safely. Good day, gentle-men. Miss Stafford," he announced as he tipped his hat and kicked his horse into motion, gliding it through the trees and out of sight in seconds. Cord immediately walked over to check on Billy with Nathan right behind him. Madeline started their way but Cord stopped her. "I need you, Holbrook and Tell to get ready to leave. Nathan, help me get Billy up on his horse."

The two men stepped over to Billy who as still grimacing in pain. "Do you think you can ride?" Cord asked him. Billy looked at Cord and nodded sharply without speaking. The two men gingerly lifted Billy and carefully walked him over and sat him up on his horse while holding him in position until he was able to take over and sit up in the saddle while leaning somewhat forward. Nathan handed him the reins. "You sure you're okay to ride?" he asked the young man. Billy nodded as he grimaced from the pain, holding the reins tightly in his hand while holding his injured shoulder with the other one. Cord and Nathan walked back to the campsite as he kicked his bedding out of the way and grabbed his gun belt from off of the ground and began buckling it while looking over at Nathan who had grabbed his own rifle.

"We've got to get moving. Now."

Frank Quincey pulled his horse up short as he stopped and listened at the same time that Red Bear did the same. "Did you hear that?" he asked out loud to the indian, who nodded in agreement.

"That sounded like a gunshot," Fox said as he, too, listened for something to follow up the sound, but there was nothing else to hear.

"It came from over there," Quincey stated as he pointed off in the direction they were heading.

"They aren't shooting at us, are they, Frank?" One of the men in the group asked.

"No," he assured him while still trying to pinpoint the origin of the shot. "If they were shooting at us there'd be a lot more shooting than that."

"Do we keep going, Frank?" Fox asked as he also continued to comb the hillside looking for any sign of movement.

"Yeah. We keep moving until someone *does* start shooting." Frank Quincey looked over at Red Bear who looked at him and nodded as he kicked his horse into motion with Quincey and his men following right behind him.

The group of men wound their way higher up into the hills as they also kept their eyes out for anyone who might be hiding above them just waiting for the opportunity to ambush them, although with being so outnumbered they doubted these people would try to take such a stand against them.

Quincey followed Red Bear's lead as they ascended higher into the hillside getting deeper into the wooded area. The terrain was beginning to open up in places forcing them to slow their pace to make sure they weren't passing by someone who might be hiding in the midst of it. Satisfied they weren't missing anything they continued scaling the hills all the while getting farther into them. It was another half-hour before Quincey picked up on something new. "I smell smoke. There's a fire nearby."

Fox raised his nose ever so slightly into the air and breathed in deeply. "Yeah. I smell it, too."

"We're close," Quincey announced as he drew his gun and cocked it, prompting the others to do the same. "Everybody keep your eyes open."

# CHAPTER SIXTEEN

They fought their way through the darkness as they hurried their escape. The going was slow and meticulous as they weaved in and out, dodging errant hidden tree limbs and brush that hung in front of them and stood in their way, tempting to claw at them as they passed through them.

Cord wanted, needed, to move faster but he accepted that, at the moment, his hands were tied from doing so. He couldn't risk pushing Billy any more than he already had given his deteriorating condition. He had no idea how bad his wound was or how long the young man could sit in a saddle. If they pushed him too hard it would be the death of him, but he dared not let up, not just yet or the young man was sure to die. As much as he hated pushing him they had no choice. He would be assured of no medical care if all of the rest of them were dead. He wished he had the option of stopping to tend to his wound, but given their circumstance that just wasn't possible.

If Quincey caught up with them he would have no mercy for any of them, much less a wounded man. At one point he had even considered giving Billy a gun and hiding him out somewhere back in the trees, well off the road and away from the possibility that Quincey would come upon him until he could make it to town and bring back help, but he feared the young man would probably not make it that long. He also feared that if Billy were left all alone out here he might consider his future to be bleak and decide he wasn't willing to suffer any longer or wait for help that might not be coming and choose to end things himself. Being the one to give him that opportunity was not something Cord could do and it was not something Cord was willing to have to live with so despite his better judgement, they continued on.

The woods were dense and unpredictable. They had been coming down in elevation which opened up the path to more trees and bushes. His only consolation was in knowing that Quincey would have just as much difficulty navigating through the terrain as they were. With the amount of horses they were moving, possibly even more.

He longed for the sun, willing it to come up faster than he was prepared to wait for it. They needed every advantage they could muster as time was not their friend at the moment. By his estimates they still had a good fifteen or so miles before they made it to Hurley, it could be less it was hard to tell while being so deep in the woods but either way it was still a ways off before they would make it there, if they made it there at all. Although he was beginning to have his doubts about it he dared not share those worries with the others. He felt as if Nathan also believed the same, even though he had never mentioned it, but it was to the man's credit that he had not spoken of such. At least for now, Cord needed the others to believe that they had a chance of making it to town in time. If it began to look as if they weren't, he would not have to inform them of such. They would be able to realize it on their own.

As they pressed on, no one spoke, the only sound to be

heard being the clomping of hooves. Cord didn't know if the silence was out of exhaustion or panic or both, but the reasoning behind it didn't matter. There was no need to express their thoughts since they were all feeling the same thing.

They continued on until they finally got a glimpse of the sun beginning to reveal itself over the far landscape, it's threads of rays slicing through the tree limbs. The sight of it was a boost to the morale and just the break they needed. They were finishing descending from the hills just as it topped the horizon directly behind them. But Cord did not have long to dwell in his jubilation since it was short-lived as he reminded himself that their advantage was also Quincey's advantage. The thought pushed him on even harder.

They were glad to see that the terrain was finally opening up even more and by the time the sun had shown itself for a full hour they experienced their first relief in quite some time as they found themselves hitting the valley floor. It was their time to put as much distance between them and Quincey as they could. Now they would see how much their horses had left in them, hopefully without killing them.

Cord pulled back often to check on Billy, the last time he did he was alarmed as to his condition. He could tell that he was having difficulty staying in the saddle. He stopped once to check his bleeding, which seemed to have slowed but, even so, it was being aggravated by the rhythmic bouncing of his horse. He could tell that it should still be considered a concern. Nathan saw Cord pulling Billy's horse over and stopped alongside the two horses to render his help.

Cord placed his hand on the side of Billy's face to see how responsive he was and then he felt his forehead and discovered that he was burning up with a fever. He pulled Billy's hand away from the wound and took a good look at it before turning to Nathan. "He's getting really shaky trying to stay in his saddle. I'll tie him in as best I can while you keep them moving. Keep the peaks on your left and head straight down the valley. We'll catch up with you as soon as we can."

"Right," Nathan said without arguing as he pulled his horse west and kicked it into motion to make it up to the rest of the group.

Cord pulled the rope from Billy's saddle and took out his pocket knife, cutting off a section of the rope. He tied Billy's hands to the pommel making sure to give him enough room to move with the motion of the running horse. When he was satisfied that he had done all he could, he touched Billy's good shoulder to get his attention. The young man slowly glanced up at Cord, barely responsive, his eyes partially shut and hollow, his expression flat and dull. Cord knew that the wounded man couldn't continue on like this for much longer. It was only a matter of time before he passed out from blood loss and shock and would not be able to be revived. He had to make a decision and he had to make it quick if he was going to have any sort of chance of saving the young man's life.

Cord slapped the rear of Billy's horse, sending it off into a gallop towards the other horses as he followed suit. It took them several minutes to catch up with them but once they had Cord pulled up alongside Nathan's horse and caught his eye. When Nathan glanced over at him Cord shook his head enough to alert him to the seriousness of Billy's situation and Nathan nodded that he understood as they continued riding.

They had gone another five or so miles when Cord motioned for them to stop in the edge of a grove of trees that sheltered them from where they had just traveled. Cord dismounted and walked over to Billy who was slumped over the pommel, his head partially hanging in front of him. When Cord checked him he was unresponsive. Nathan and Madeline also came up behind him to check on him and Cord motioned for him to help him untie him and slide him gently down from his horse and onto the grass.

"How is he?" Madeline asked softly, her face masked with worry as she wiped the young man's forehead with her handkerchief.

Cord shook his head in anguish as he focused on the young man's deteriorating health. "He's lost a lot of blood. I think he's going into shock. He can't keep up like this," he said as Holbrook and Tell also walked up behind them and watched in silence.

"How is young William?" Holbrook asked.

"He's not doing well," Madeline offered to answer as she glanced over at him.

"Is there anything we can do for him?" Tell asked with genuine uncertainty.

"I don't know what that would be," Cord answered without looking up. He stood and looked at Madeline and Nathan as he motioned with his head over to the side away from the others. As he stepped a few feet over out of the way where Billy couldn't hear them, they followed. "We can't keep doing this," he stated bluntly to the two as they each looked at him.

"What are we going to do?" Madeline asked.

"I don't know. All I know is he won't make it if we keep trying to force him to ride."

"I'll stay behind with him," Nathan suggested boldly.

"No," Cord disagreed. "I will."

"You have to stay with Madeline and them," Nathan exclaimed as he motioned over to Tell and Holbrook.

"Don't use me to try to make your point," Madeline snipped at the logic. "I can take care of myself."

"I know you can," Nathan responded as he tried to take back the insinuation. "That wasn't about you."

"Cord, you know you can't stay behind," Madeline pointed out. "You know the way."

"Nathan, you can't stay. I can't have you do that."

"It's my choice, Cord," Nathan assured him. "Besides, if we hide out, Quincy's likely to pass us by and keep going after you."

"But what if he doesn't? He'll kill you. I won't take that chance."

"You won't have to," they heard Tell announce from behind them. "Billy's dead."


The horse carrying River Holloway passed through a small canyon and had just entered a thicket when he decided he needed to stop for a bit so he held up under some low hanging branches that would provide some cover for him. He had put several hours between he and the others with no sign of them or Frank Quincey or any of his men following him, allowing him the chance to relax for the first time since he had left the others.

River removed his Stetson and wiped the side of his face with the sleeve of his coat before swinging down from the saddle and tying his horse to one of the tree branches at his disposal. He decided he had come far enough that he could take the time to stretch his legs and take a short rest before he continued on his journey.

The sun had risen enough that it was beating down on him now, heating him up to the point that he had grown uncomfortable in his coat. He slipped it off and tossed it onto the ground next to him as he reveled in the instant relief. He took a long drink from his canteen as he surveyed the path in front of him. Although being somewhat unfamiliar with the area he still had a basic idea of where he was and by his rough estimates he would be able to make it to Maysville sometime around dark.

Happy with how things had turned out for him he wanted to take in his good fortune and tugged on the knotted rope to release the payroll bags that it held in place until one of them was loosened enough for him to remove it from the saddle. Taking the bag, he sat down at the base of the tree and exhaled deeply in relief. He wondered about how he would safely travel with so much cash. A smile formed on his face as he unbuckled the strap on the bag and opened it.

Just as abruptly, his smile instantly dropped as he glanced down into the bag full of charts, blueprints and other types of railroad papers. Panic flooded over him as he desperately dug deeper into the bag only to uncover more of the papers from Holbrook's satchel with several large rocks lining the bottom of the bag to give it added weight. Dumbfounded by the discovery he jumped up and grabbed the remaining three bags from the saddle and dropped to the ground on his knees as he feverishly unbuckled each bag individually only to find that each one contained nothing but more papers and rocks.

He sat, unable to speak, his mouth hung open from the shock as the realization of the deception set in. It took him several minutes of sitting there for him to accept what had happened to him as he sat back against the tree, his mind rolling about in a blur. He felt a burst of anger hit him as he screamed out in anger and threw the last bag he had been holding as far as he could out in front of him and leaned his head back against the tree, closing his eyes in disgust and aggravation at his apparent ignorance.

"Well done, Mr. Chantry," he spoke softly under his breath. "Well done, indeed."

# CHAPTER SEVENTEEN

The statement of Billy's passing brought silence to Cord, Nathan and Madeline with everyone unable to utter a word. They glanced at one another and walked over to where Billy Richmond lay, each of them staring down at his lifeless body, wrapped in shock at what had just happened. Cord squatted next to the young man and hopelessly placed his hand on the side of his neck to feel for a pulse, but there was none. He took his hand away and gently bowed his head out of respect and saddened by the loss of such a young man so innocent in all of this.

Billy had been so young, exactly how young he had not known, a thought that he now regretted and which strangely angered him because he had not known him long enough to even find out. At first he wondered if he even had any family and then remembered that Billy had mentioned an uncle in Benton Springs who had the ranch that he was going to work on. He would need to get in touch with the man and inform him of what had happened with his nephew. It was not the sort of news he was looking forward to sharing with the man, but it was the least he could do for him. He owed that much to Billy.

He softly patted Billy on the chest and then stood. "Help me get him up on my horse," Cord said to the group as he reached down to pick him up. Nathan and Tell helped Cord carry Billy over to the Shire and laid him across its back using the rope they had secured him to the saddle with to tie his hands underneath. Once he was satisfied he was secured, Cord swung up into the saddle on Billy's horse and pulled his revolver as he checked to make sure there were rounds in the chambers. All of this was witnessed by Madeline as the curiosity of it caught her attention.

"What do you think you're doing?" she asked with concern as she walked over to his horse.

Cord ignored the question and instead turned to address Nathan. "Stay on this trail for about another ten miles or so and it'll take you straight into Hurley."

Madeline defiantly stepped in front of his horse before he could move and grabbed the horse's reins as she glared at him. "I asked you a question."

Cord looked at her sternly, unfazed by her stance. "I'm going after River," he stated bluntly as he holstered his gun and the looked back at her, his eyes without expression.

"Are you *crazy?*" she asked sharply. "I'm as upset as you are over losing Billy, but this isn't how you deal with it. You can't go after him right now. You can't do that. We have to get to Hurley."

"No, *you* have to get to Hurley. *I'm* going to kill River."

"But we *all* have to go. That was the deal," she argued.

"What would you have me to do?" Cord snapped. "Let him get away with murdering that innocent boy?'

"We need you to get us to Hurley, Cord."

"Nathan can get you there," he insisted as he tried to pull the reins away from her grasp, but she only tightened her grip on them even more. "Let go," he demanded as he looked down at her.

"No. May I remind you that we have a lunatic and his men who are trying to hunt us down and kill us?"

"No, you don't have to remind me which is why if you leave now you can stay ahead of them until you get to Hurley. The sheriff will take over from there and help you. I'll get there as soon as I can once I find River and take care of things. Now, let go of my horse."

"That's a fancy way of saying you're going to hunt him down and kill him, isn't it?" she stated.

"So what if I am? What does it matter?"

"Because if you do this then you're no better than Frank Quincey and what he intends to do. You'll be hunting down a man for killing someone they knew."

"Don't worry about me. I'll be fine going after him alone."

"No, if you go after him all you're going to do is end up getting yourself killed, if not by River then by Quincey and his men."

"I know what I'm doing," Cord stated flatly as he pulled on the reins impatiently.

Madeline continued to hold onto them preventing his leaving. "Do you? Because it doesn't sound like you do. So what if you go after him and you catch up with him and kill him, then what? Do you honestly think that's going to bring Billy back?"

"No, but..."

"Is that what you think he would want you to do?"

Cord's expression showed his irritation, his face set in grim, watchful lines. "He would want me to find his killer and rid the world of him so he couldn't hurt anyone else," he said as his patience grew slim. "I owe that to him so his death wasn't for nothing. It's what Billy would want."

"No, he wouldn't," she argued. "Billy looked up to you. He

would want you to do what you set out to do and that's to get all of us safely to Hurley."

"Well, it's a little late for that now, isn't it? I was supposed to get *all* of you there, not just *most* of you!"

"There's nothing you can do about that now, Cord. It wasn't your fault! Stop blaming yourself for something you couldn't control! This was all River's doing. It had nothing to do with you. He drew on River. He took the chance and he lost."

"She's right, Cord," Nathan added as he walked over closer to them. "Don't do this. You aren't going to do anybody any good if you're dead."

"But he can't get away with this," Cord exclaimed as his mood somewhat softened.

"He won't get away with it," Nathan insisted. "We'll make sure he pays for it, but not by your hands, but by the law. And not by you going after him alone. You don't know how dangerous he is. You already know he'll kill without provocation. "

Cord was frustrated and full of anger, but he knew there was a ring of truth to what they was saying. He would see justice brought to River, maybe not today but one day soon. As long as he had breath left in him he would make sure of that. He looked down at Madeline who nodded silently in agreement.

Suddenly, Tell spoke up from behind them. "I don't mean to interrupt or sound insensitive, but shouldn't we be going?"

The mass of horses barreled down onto the valley as if in one motion, their pace picking up as soon as they made it out onto flatter ground. They had time to make up and there was no time to waste. It wouldn't be long before the ones they were after would be in Hurley. Once that happened they would have to go through the law there in order to get to them, the law of Sage Connelly, a thought that Frank Quincey did not take lightly. What he had heard about the man's reputation was enough to discourage Quincey from ever setting foot in the man's town. It was trouble than he did not need. But now he had been forced into that task, a task that Frank Quincey did not look forward to and preferred not to have to deal with, if at all possible. He needed to catch up with these people before he had that to worry over.

The sound of thundering hooves filled the valley as the group continued on. It was no longer necessary for Red Bear to check for tracks as it was apparent where Cord and the others were going. They were headed to Hurley.

Frank Quincey could savor the sweet taste of revenge getting closer as they moved along. At any moment he hoped to look up and see them in front of him, running for their lives but losing out just short of salvation. He would take great pleasure in watching them all die, one by one he would take them out, each one would die knowing that it was all because of what they had done to Virgil. It would not bring him back, but it would be a fitting end to the murdering scum. Then he could return to Benton Springs and sleep well tonight knowing that they had been appropriately dealt with.

As they were riding along, Fox pulled up next to Frank Quincey's horse and leaned over to shout at him. "Shouldn't we stop for a bit and rest the horses? We've been pushing them pretty hard."

"No," Quincey adamantly refused. "We keep after them. If they don't stop, then we don't stop!"

"But Frank, the horses are done for! We can't keep pushing them like this!"

"I said we're not stopping!" he declared as he turned back towards the path in front of them, putting his head down to steer the wind away from his face as much as possible. He was a man on a mission and nothing was going to get in his way. *Nothing.*

The sound of a round being chambered into the winchester caught Deputy Tom Wills attention as he walked through the door and into the sheriff's office. Sheriff Sage Connelly had just finished loading the rifle and was starting on loading the Greener double-barrel shotgun with buckshot. Deputy Wills walked over to the gun rack and pulled down another Greener and began loading it, too, before stuffing a handful of extra shells into his vest pocket.

Deputy Wills glanced over at Sheriff Connelly silently admiring his courage. The man was no stranger to a fight and never seemed to let the anticipation of getting into one deter him. He had no idea how many such skirmishes Connelly had been in since pinning on a badge, but he had never heard of the man coming out on the losing end of one. He did not anticipate this one ending any differently.

"Are you going to deputize anyone else, sheriff?" Deputy Wills asked.

"No," Connelly stated calmly. "We don't need to get any innocent people involved in this if we don't have to. It's not their fight and it's going to get messy so I don't want anyone else's blood on my hands."

Deputy Tom Wills hesitated, thinking back to what Sheriff Connelly had told him about those headed their way, about there being at least six and possibly as many as a dozen or more men that had taken the money from the stage. They had killed the driver and the foreman so it was obvious that they had not qualms over taking innocent lives. In the midst of them could be passengers from the stage that may, or may not, have been in on the robbery so they wouldn't know right off hand who to trust and who to be leery of until they confronted them. It was a vague description of what was coming their way and when it came to dealing with those breaking the law Sheriff Connelly didn't care for vague. He had seen Connelly deal with hardened criminals before and he had no doubt that the man could do it again, despite the overwhelming odds.

"Do we know when they'll get here?" Deputy Wills asked as he laid his own Winchester down on the desk to get cartridges.

"The sheriff of Jackson Springs didn't say, but judging from when he sent the telegram and when the robbery took place it could be sometime today or even tomorrow at the latest, depending on how fast they ride."

"How do you want to handle this?"

"They'll be coming in on the west end of town so I'll have you posted at the livery stable and I'll be in the freight office. We'll be able to see them coming from a good distance so it'll give us time to see how many we're up against and to clear the streets of bystanders.

"What if there's too many of them, sheriff?"

"We'll make do," he answered. Deputy Wills wasn't exactly sure what that meant, but he had always been able to trust Sheriff Connelly and had never had to question his logic before so he decided to put his trust in the man that he wasn't getting in over his head.

"Take a spot inside the stables and keep an eye out and make sure Cookie gets out of there."

"Are we even sure they're coming this way?"

"We're the closest town from where the stage was robbed. If they're bold enough to rob a stage they aren't going to care about whatever the law is in town. Don't worry. They'll come."

# CHAPTER EIGHTEEN

Nathan felt the whip of the bullet passing right by his head a split second before he heard the shot from behind them that produced it. He instinctively ducked before he heard the multiple shots that followed it all of them too close for him to ignore. He and Cord looked back at the same time to see Frank Quincey and his men bearing down on them of in the distance, the smoke from their shots drifting off into the air. The eruption of gunfire caught Madeline's attention, too, causing her to glance back at their followers and being able to see them and to gasp at how close they were. They were still off in the distance, too far back to have any sort of accuracy, but there were so many of them shooting that there was still the chance that one of the bullets might accidentally hit one of them. It was the first time any of them had seen who was trying to kill them.

"Keep 'em moving!" Cord yelled out to Nathan, who was riding beside him. Before Nathan could respond, Cord pulled his horse up and fell back taking refuge behind a small outcrop of boulders on the valley floor that they had just passed. Nathan watched him jump down from his horse right next to the rock formation holding his rifle and ducking behind the rocks readying for the men's arrival. Cord was about to take aim when he heard a horse behind him. He whirled around leveling the rifle at his waist anticipating that some of Quincey's men had somehow flanked around him and was coming up from behind. He was shocked to see Nathan jumping down from his horse. His surprise was interrupted by a bullet tearing a chunk of rock from the boulder hiding him as tiny fragments peppered his neck, drawing his attention back to the riders. As he turned back to face their approach Nathan came up next to him ducking down behind the rocks.

"I told you to get them into town!" he snapped as he readied his rifle.

"What, and let you have all the fun?" Nathan declared as he, too, took aim.

Cord looked over at the man and threw him a smile which was met by one from Nathan. They both turned back to the riders who were still almost a mile out.

"What do you say?" Cord suggested. "I take the ones on the right and you go for the ones on the left?"

"Sounds good," Nathan replied calmly as he took careful aim.

Cord took aim as well. "Well, let's give it to 'em." Each man held their rifles on the nearest rider and fired.

As two of Quincey's men toppled from their horses, a shocked Frank Quincey pulled his horse short and darted off to the side to the nearest grove of trees with his men behind him, but not before Cord and Nathan took down two more of them before they could reach cover. Quincey jumped down from his horse and darted behind a tree without even taking the time to tie it off. He looked over at the dead men lying out in the grass and cursed loudly. He was about to say something to the men when a bullet picked a chunk of bark out of the tree he was hiding behind just above his head, forcing him to duck behind it.

"Frank!" one of his men called out in desperation.

"What?!"

"What do we do? They've got us pinned down!"

"Take four men with you and circle off to the left. Try to get off to the side of them!"

He watched as the man motioned to others to follow behind him as they disappeared into the thicket skirting wide around the trees to get a better vantage point. "Let's give 'em some cover!" Quincey yelled as the shooting began in order to draw Cord and Nathan's attention away from what was happening

Cord and Nathan were suddenly flooded with bullets, causing both to duck behind the boulders and wait for the shooting to die down. Cord crouched down sideways with his left shoulder pressed tightly against the boulder and facing the trees off to their side and was waiting for a chance to return fire when he saw movement.

"We've got company!"

"No kidding, "Nathan responded sarcastically as he continued occasionally getting off a shot during the barrage of gunfire.

"On your right!" Cord yelled as he repositioned his firing over to the side. He could see multiple men slipping through the trees and coming their way, just how many there were he was unsure. He held his rifle in the vicinity of the men coming around the side until he had a clear shot at one of them and fired. A man called out as he was hit to the surprise of the others who were caught off guard by the shot and froze in their steps just long enough for Cord to squeeze off another shot resulting in another of Quincey's men being struck in the side. The man fell to the ground and started desperately clawing his way across the grass until two of the other men revealed themselves from their cover and grabbed the wounded man by the arms and dragged him over behind the nearest tree as the others with him fired back to cover his rescue.

Cord ducked behind a smaller boulder facing the side and waited.

"How much longer are we planning on staying?" Nathan asked in a joking tone, but meant with seriousness.

Cord tried to answer him but a bullet ricocheted off the boulder above his head before he could, temporarily distracting him and interrupting his train of thought for a few brief seconds. He waited to ensure another bullet wouldn't be any closer before he tried again to speak. "I want to give Madeline and the others as much time as possible to get to Hurley."

"Then what?"

"Then we get to the horses and make a run for it."

"You got any more ideas?"

"Why? What's wrong with that one?"

"Nothing, except the part where we get a back full of lead while we're leaving. I can't see your friends here just letting us ride off without having something to say about it."

"Well, I'm open for suggestions," Cord said as he glanced over the tops of the boulders and got off a few more shots. He turned back to the side and caught a glimpse of one of the remaining men repositioning to a tree closer to them. As the man stepped out into the clearing between trees Cord dropped him with a shot, wounding him. When the man raised his injured body up off of the ground to try to move to cover, Cord pumped another round into him. This time, the man did not move again. Cord turned and slid down with his back against the rocks. "Still waiting on that plan of yours!" he announced.

"I'm thinking!" Nathan shouted over the gunfire as he returned a few more shots of his own.

"Well, you'd better think of something quick because we can't stay here!"

"Alright, you go and I'll cover you!" Nathan suggested as he stayed down behind the rocks.

"No!" Cord argued. "We go together or we don't go at all!"

"We'll never make it going together!"

"Then I'm staying here until you go!"

"Has anybody ever told you that you're hard headed?!"

"Yeah, and I didn't listen then, either!"

"Fine, we'll do it your way!" Nathan conceded while bobbing his head up for one more shot.

"You reload first," Cord announced as he took an occasional shot just to keep them preoccupied. As he continued to fire intermittently, Nathan pulled cartridges from his gun belt and reloaded his rifle. When he was finished, he called out to signal Cord. "Done!"

The two men switched duties and Cord started reloading as Nathan fired a shot to keep the men busy until Cord announced that he was finished. "Done!"

"How do we do this?" Nathan asked, genuinely concerned to hear the response.

"You saddle up first while I cover for you and then you cover me."

"How will you know when I've made it to my horse?"

"When I hear you start shooting, I'll know to run!"

"If you don't hear any shots..."

"I will," Cord confidently cut him off and looking over at him before he could finish. Nathan understood his meaning and nodded simply without needing to speak.

"Let me know when you're ready," Cord instructed him as he fired again several times. He watched out of the corner of his eye until Nathan turned with his back against the boulders in a squatting position, his rifle firmly grasped in his left hand. He looked over at Cord, but said nothing as a wave of uncertainty flooding over his face. Cord looked at his friend with intensity. "Good luck," he said calmly to Nathan as he followed it with a faint smile.

"You, too."

Cord popped his head up just long enough to assess the others before positioning himself. "Ready?"

"Ready!" Nathan said.

"Go!" shouted Cord as Nathan made a run for his horse. As soon as Nathan started to move, Cord popped up from behind his hiding position and began firing repeatedly in rapid succession, first at Quincey and the cluster of his men and then spinning around and laying out several shots at the men off to his right without taking the time to carefully aim and without stopping, pumping out shots as fast as the winchester would fire. He switched back once again and returned more fire to the men in front of them and then took a few more shots off to his side. A second later, he heard Nathan's first shot. With adrenaline pumping through his body and without hesitation, he jumped up and made a run for it.

Nathan was on his horse firing wildly with his rifle between the two groups of men while his horse began nervously jumping around and stepping about in half-circles from the sounds of all the shooting and causing Nathan to have to switch from side to side in order to continue facing their adversaries. He watched as Cord continued running towards his horse until he was a few feet away for it when he saw Cord's body buckle as a bullet struck him in the leg.

Cord grunted from the pain and dropped his rifle as he fell to the ground. Nathan continued firing back as he edged his horse forward placing himself between Cord and Quincey's men while still firing away to give Cord more time to recover, grab his rifle and get up onto his horse. Cord struggled to get to his feet while the bullets continued flying past him. With a bullet lodged in his left leg he was forced to go around to the other side of his horse and try to climb into the stirrups on the right side. Nathan continued firing to give him cover with Cord struggling until he was finally able to swing his leg into the saddle just as Nathan's rifle emptied. Nathan quickly tossed it to the ground and pulled his revolver as Cord simultaneously pulled his revolver and began firing, too. The two men pulled their reins away in the direction behind them and kicked their horses into motion.

As they hurried away from Quincey and his men a bullet hit Nathan in the left arm, throwing it forward with such force that he almost dropped his gun from his right hand. They rode away as fast as their horses would take them, wounded and spent as they listened to the shots continuing behind them, hearing the whipping sound of some as they passed right by them. They had only been riding for a few seconds when Cord looked back at Nathan and saw that he was hurt as blood covered the lower half of his arm. He started to drop back to check on him but Nathan motioned for him to keep moving. Cord looked back to the front, grimacing from the pain radiating from his leg and longing for the sight of Hurley, thankful to be able to put the shootout behind them for the time being while also facing the reality that it was far from over.

# CHAPTER NINETEEN

Sheriff Sage Connelly watched as four horses galloped into Hurley in a sea of dust. Sheriff Connelly poised his shotgun, bracing for a potential fight, but as soon as he saw the riders he realized that they did not appear to pose a threat. Likewise, Deputy Tom Wills did the same, taking the sheriff's lead and withdrawing his weapon that had been pointed at the approaching riders.

The townspeople who were on the west end of town glanced up with surprise as three horses carrying Madeline, Holbrook and Tell galloped into Hurley pulling a Shire with the dead body of Billy Richmond tied across its back. The commotion they created brought others from the various buildings out onto the boardwalks and streets to see who had ascended upon their town with such haste. The four horses came to a stop, not mistakenly in front of the sheriff's office. Holbrook remained on his horse while holding the reins of the Shire while Madeline and Tell dismounted and were heading for the sheriff's door when he called out to them as he continued walking down the boardwalk towards them.

"Hold it right there," he announced as he cautiously held

the shotgun pointed in front of him but down towards the ground while he walked the remaining distance over to them. "If you're looking for the sheriff, you just found him."

Caught off guard, Madeline turned her attention in his direction. "Sheriff, we were on the stage that was robbed," she blurted out anxiously.

Sheriff Connelly lowered his weapon and finished the walk over to them. "You talking about the stage between Jackson Creek and Benton Springs?"

"Yes," she answered as she pulled back the stray strands of hair that had fallen down onto the side of her face and tucked them behind her ear.

"Are you the only ones who made it?" Sheriff Connelly asked as Deputy Tom Wills walked up behind the trio.

"No, there are two more of us. There's a group of men that were after the payroll on the stage that were after us. The other two men that were with us stayed behind to hold them off long enough for us to escape."

"Did they make it out?"

Madeline's expression sank from the possibility that she couldn't and didn't want to imagine. "I...I don't know, sheriff."

Sheriff Connelly looked the group over and decided he could trust what she was telling him. "Where are your friends now?"

"They were a few miles behind us."

Sheriff Connelly threw Deputy Tom Wills a hard look. "We need to get everybody out of town. They need to go out to the church and stay there until this thing is over."

"You got it, sheriff," Deputy Tom Wills declared.

"I'll help him," Tell volunteered.

"Get going. We don't have much time," Sheriff Connelly said, sending the men away to do their task. Deputy Tom Wills and Tell had started going into businesses warning them that they had to leave and head up to the church for safety as

Sheriff Connelly continued talking with Madeline with Holbrook standing close.

"So, what were you saying about these men?"

Madeline continued. "The men caught up with us and our friends stayed behind to give us a chance to make it here with the money."

The comment caught his attention. "You mean you have the payroll money with you?"

"Yes, it's in our saddlebags."

"So I take it these men are on their way here to get the money?"

"Yes, I believe so and also to kill us for shooting their friends during the holdup. They've been following us since we left the stage so I can't imagine that they would be willing to give up on it now."

"If that's the case then we need to get it over to the bank before they make it here. How many men are we talking about?"

"I'm not sure, but somewhere between fifteen and twenty."

The figure was daunting to hear, especially since it was only he and Deputy Wills there to protect the town, but there was nothing the sheriff could do about that except to brace for their arrival. Madeline had said her two friends had remained behind to hold them off, but that would only slow down their arrival. With just two guns against that large of a group of men they didn't stand much of a chance, if any, although he wasn't going to admit that out loud to them, even though he had to assume that they already knew it. Their standoff wouldn't stop the onslaught of the men, but merely delay it possibly by minutes only. Once her friends were dead, the group of men wouldn't be far behind.

"We don't have long. Would you mind getting the payroll out for me? It'll be a lot easier to protect if it's in the bank vault." Sheriff Connelly asked as he motioned for Deputy Wills to assist her.

Madeline and Tell turned and stepped back over to the horses and removed the saddlebags from all three horses as Sheriff Connelly noticed Billy Richmond's body tied over the Shire. "Is that one of the passengers of the stage?"

Madeline glanced over at Billy's body. "Yes, he was on the stage. One of the other passengers tried to steal the money from us. Billy tried to stop him and he shot him."

"Wait. One of the other passengers was part of the gang that was robbing the stage?"

"No, he tried to take the money from us while we were on our way here to turn it in."

"I'll need any information you have on him, but I'll get that from you later. Right now, we need to hurry up and get this money over to the bank before those men hit town."

Tell helped Deputy Wills had just returned from notifying the townspeople and helped carry the saddlebags over to the bank while Sheriff Connelly, Madeline and Holbrook walked with them. Sheriff Connelly warned the bank president about what was coming and that they didn't have time to relay all of the events of what had happened to them right then. The bank president secured the money inside the vault as they quickly walked back outside.

"I need the three of you to go hide in my office till this is over. You'll be safe there. When the shooting starts, stay in there, no matter what you hear. Deputy Wills and I will be..."

Sheriff Connelly was interrupted by the sound of horses running into town. He turned sharply to glance in the direction and saw two riders approaching at a full gallop. He started to raise his gun, but Madeline called out to stop him when she recognized them.

"No!" she shouted. "They're with us!"

Sheriff Connelly lowered his gun and he and the others

walked briskly over to the two riders as they stopped outside his office next to their horses. They were just dismounting by the time they made it over to them. Madeline saw the blood covering most of the sleeve of Nathan's left arm, but before she could comment Cord had climbed down from his saddle and she noticed that he was limping as she saw the blood.

"They're coming," Cord declared to the group before anyone who speak as he limped around the back of the horses.

"I'm Sheriff Connelly," the sheriff stated as he nodded a welcome.

"Cord Chantry, and this here's Nathan Brooks," Cord said as he motioned to Nathan.

Sheriff Connelly nodded at Nathan, as well, ignoring their wounds for the time being. "How far out are they?"

"They're right behind us," Cord said as he tried to balance himself on his good leg as he pulled his handkerchief from around his neck and delicately tied it around the wound, seething through his teeth from the pain it generated. "I give 'em five, maybe ten minutes at the most."

Madeline had walked over to Nathan and carefully checked his wound as he flinched from her touch. "Sorry. It looks like the bullet went through." She looked at him. "Can you move it?"

Nathan shook his head. "It's broken."

Deputy Wills and Tell had walked up to the group, having gotten the word started notifying all of the townspeople to leave town and waited for the sheriff's instructions.

"Tom, go get Doc Reynolds to have him look at both of them," Sheriff Connelly suggested. But before the deputy could make a move, Cord spoke up.

"Sheriff, we don't have time. Those men will be here any minute. You've got to get the rest of these people out of here before it's too late."

"He's right," Sheriff Connelly agreed. "Tom, clear the streets. I'll take this young lady and her friends inside my office." Deputy Tom Wills turned and called out to the townspeople who had stopped what they were doing and were staring at the spectacle that was unfolding in front of them. "Alright! Everybody to the church! Let's go! Move it!" he demanded. He watched as the rest of the residents started scurrying from the nearest buildings and headed towards the church without complaints before he turned back to help Sheriff Connelly while Madeline and Holbrook walked towards the sheriff's office. Tell stayed behind with the others.

"You need to go inside till this thing is over," Cord told Tell, who was standing next to him.

"You need my help, Cord," the young man stated.

"I'm not going to take a chance of you getting shot like Billy," Cord argued.

"That's not your call, Cord. You need my help and you know it."

Cord wanted to argue the point, but he could tell that the man wasn't going to back down. "Alright," Cord reluctantly agreed, "but you stay hidden, got it?"

Tell nodded as he loosened his gun in its holster before he looked over at Sheriff Connelly. "Where do you want me, sheriff?"

"Well, first, come in my office and get a rifle," Sheriff Connelly suggested, "and then take a spot up there behind the saloon sign," he said as he pointed across the street to the building. The spot was ideal since it gave him a clear view of anyone who would be coming into town, but was still large enough to give him adequate cover.

"Tom? Keep an eye out and once you see them coming head over to the livery stables. I'll put Cord over there in the freight office so he'll be close and I'll take the spot between the land office and the undertaker," Sheriff Connelly said as Tom walked outside and into the edge of the street, watching for movement out in the distance. Cord, Tell and Nathan walked into the office where Cord and Tell took two of the rifles from the gun rack and began filling them for a box of cartridges that Sheriff Connelly had retrieved from a desk drawer. Madeline had Nathan sit down and was applying a makeshift sling around his neck to help stabilize his arm while Holbrook stood back and watched.

"We've got to hurry up and get in position," Cord pointed out. "Quincey will be here any minute now."

The comment caught Sheriff Connelly's attention, causing him to stop loading a rifle and look over at Cord. "Did you say '*Quincey*'? Do you mean *Frank Quincey?*"

"Yeah," Cord answered as he stopped loading his own rifle and glanced up at the man. "Have you heard of him?"

"Yeah, unfortunately. He's been terrorizing the people of Benton Springs for several years now. I knew eventually he'd find a reason to make his way over here. He's bad news."

"We found that out," Cord said as he finished with his rifle and chambered a round.

"This young lady said there were between fifteen and twenty of them. Is that about right?"

"Originally yeah, but there's about five or six less of them now."

"Good," Sheriff Connelly said as he nodded. We need the numbers as much in our favor as possible. Are you going to be alright?" He asked while pointing down at Cord's injured leg.

"As long as I don't have to do a lot of walking or any running."

"I'll set you up there in the doorway of the freight office with some boxes of cartridges. That way, if you need more ammo you'll have access to it."

"Thanks, sherif," Cord spoke with a simple nod.

"Where do you want me, sheriff?" Nathan questioned as he tried to stand, but sheriff Connelly placed his hand gently on his shoulder to stop him from doing so.

"You need to stay put."

"At least give me a revolver," Nathan requested. "I've still got one good arm."

"But it's only six shots," Sheriff Connelly stated. "What happens when you're empty?"

"I'll reload it for him," Holbrook offered bravely.

"Alright, but all of you aren't to get out in the open, understand?"

The three of them nodded as Nathan handed his revolver to Madeline who went to work emptying and reloading shells.

Sheriff Connelly picked up the Greener and looked over at Cord. "If things go sour..."

"Sheriff!" they heard Deputy Wills call from out on the street. "They're coming!"

# CHAPTER TWENTY

The dust created by the movement of the horses drifted off into the distance as the riders headed straight for town, their sights set on a combination of robbery and revenge.

Deputy Tom Will's warning caused everyone in the sheriff's office to scramble and sent Deputy Wills over to the livery stable. Cord hobbled across the street into the freight office, taking position just inside the front door while Tell scaled the side of the saloon up to the roof where he squatted behind the large sign with a perfect view of the street below. Sheriff Connelly was the last to leave to go to the spacing between the land office and the undertaker. Nathan used the barrel of his revolver to break out one of the windows in the sheriff's office with the door locked and Holbrook and Madeline standing by to reload his revolver plus the extra one that Sheriff Connelly had given him to switch out while the other one was being loaded.

Each of the four men were in position when the riders came into view at the edge of town, their guns drawn and their horses running hard. Cord was about to open fire when it caught his attention that there were only seven or eight men riding into town. *Where were the rest of them?* He paused for only a second before it hit him. *They're coming in from the other end of town!*

Cord needed to warn the others, but with everyone spread out and already in their places it was too late to do anything about it now. He had to hope that they would each realize it, too, before it was too late.

Tom and Cord were the first to have clear shots and opened fire on the group sending one man to the ground and dropping another one off of his horse, but only wounding him. The injured man managed to crawl over to the end of the corral where he took up position behind a watering trough and began firing at Deputy Wills inside the door of the stables. Cord continued firing away as the riders jumped off of their horses and began dispersing to the nearest build-ings for cover.

One of the riders went around the back of the livery stables and tried to come in through the back door, causing Deputy Wills to have to abandon covering the front of the stables and focus on the man coming up behind him. Cord saw one of the men firing at him while the man rode around the end of the freight office to try to come around through the back. Cord repositioned himself facing the rear door, but no one immediately came through it. He tried to keep an eye on the front as he also covered the back of the freight office as best he could, but there was so many containers in his way that he couldn't get a clear view of the back door. Try as he must he was still unable to see past the large crates and supplies that were stacked up in his line of sight. He was just about to start making his way to the back of the office to find the rider who had circled around the building when he heard Tell calling out from up on the roof of the saloon confirming his worst fear. "Riders in the east!"

Just as Tell called out the warning, more riders came

around the corner building at the east end of town, their guns drawn as they rode in to find no one covering that end of Hurley. Sheriff Connelly heard Tell shout out the warning and abandoned his spot to slide between the two buildings where he had taken refuge and turned the back corner heading to the other end of town to meet this new group of riders.

Cord hid behind several large bales of cotton inside the freight office as he waited. Because of the close quarters his rifle would not be of use so he laid it down onto the floor, choosing instead to engage the man with his revolver. He drew the weapon and sat quietly and listened for movement in the back of the store. His patience finally paid off when he heard one of the wooden floor boards creak towards the back of the building, signaling that the man was inside.

Cord sat still and quietly as he waited for the sounds of any other movements. When the next floor board squeaked much closer to him, Cord took aim at the blind spot in front of him and waited. He saw the shadow of a man creeping his way farther into the office and waited until the man appeared as he fired two shots, hitting him with both and dropping him face down. After he made sure the man was dead he hobbled over to the front door and looked out onto the street. He could see Nathan still firing intermittently at several men who were trying to advance farther down the street towards the jail, but neither Sheriff Connelly or Deputy Wills were anywhere to be seen.

Tell diverted his attention over to the other end of town. He tried picking off some of this new group of riders, but they were still too far out for him to get a clean shot so he continued focusing on the first group that was advancing deeper into town.

When Cord looked out the front window of the freight office he could see that one of Quincey's men had gathered at the front of the livery stable to help the wounded man hiding behind the watering trough. After he checked on him he started to make his way over to the front door of the stables, with Deputy Wills inside unaware that another man was approaching. Cord had heard shooting from inside the stables, but had not seen the deputy within the last couple of minutes, which worried him. Once he found himself surrounded he would have very few places to hide. He needed help.

Cord opened the door of the freight office and glanced up and down the boardwalk and then the street, but there were none of Quincey's men in sight. It looked as if Quincey and his men were going from building to building looking for Cord and the others. Quincey was no fool. He would assume that the money had already been taken to the bank, which would be his last stop after killing Cord and the other passengers. Since he had no idea which one of them had killed his brother he would be forced to kill them all, which would not be a problem for him to do, that Cord was sure of. Once he had made sure all of them were dead, including Sheriff Connelly and Deputy Wills, they would take the bank with no one around to stop them knowing that there would be none of the townspeople who dared oppose them.

Cord glanced up at Tell firing from behind the saloon sign and waved to get his attention. When Tell looked over at him, Cord motioned that he was going over to the livery stables. Tell acknowledged his plan with a wave and returned to shooting as Cord started limping across the street as quickly as his wounded leg would allow him. Cord had only made it thirty feet out from the freight office when he realized he had been so focused on helping Deputy Wills that he had forgotten about the wounded man hiding behind the watering trough. He was reminded of it when the man stuck his head out from behind the trough and began firing at Cord, causing Cord to dive onto the ground, his only defense.

He laid flat trying to raise his head just enough to get a clear shot at the man but he was having trouble seeing him. He fired blindly in the man's vicinity, hoping he would get lucky but judging from the continued firing being placed upon him he wasn't having any success.

Suddenly, he saw the man's torso fall over onto the ground, lifeless. Cord rolled onto his back and saw Tell still pointing his rifle at the man to make sure he was actually dead. When he saw Cord look at him, he gave him a wave and a smile as Cord waved back. Cord then climbed to his feet and started again towards the stables to help Deputy Wills. When he had made it to the front door of the stables, he stuck his head inside the partially opened door and ducked around inside. The shooting from within distracted Quincey's man long enough for Cord to make it over to the first stall.

Cord stood in the stall for a few seconds to check the interior of the stables, but it was hard to distinguish who was doing the shooting or where Deputy Wills was and he didn't want to take a chance of accidentally firing on him or being shot by Wills himself so he was forced to stand and watch for something telling him of the deputy's location. He saw someone moving in a stall near the middle of the stables and took aim, waiting for the person to show themselves better in the dim lighting. When Cord saw that it was one of Quincey's men he called out to him.

"Hey!"

The man spun as he fired, the bullet narrowly missing Cord's head as he steadied his hand and fired. He watched as the man clutched his chest and fell into the hay. Cord then glanced down towards the back of the stables, but could not see Deputy Wills.

"Wills!"

"Yeah!" the deputy called out. A few seconds later, Cord saw the man emerge from the back of the stables with his gun still drawn. When he saw that it was Cord he holstered his weapon and walked over to him.

"Thanks," he said with a grin. "I've been pinned down by that guy for the longest!"

"Where's the sheriff?"

"I haven't seen him," Cord responded.

"We'd better go find him."

"There's another group of men that came in the other end of town."

"They're trying to bottle us in," Deputy Wills stated as he started for the front door with Cord right behind him.

Sheriff Connelly had made it across the backs of several buildings when he ran into two of Quincey's men who had already been sent around the back of the buildings to surprise whomever was in the sheriff's office while he and the others that were with him started clearing the closer buildings one at a time. When Sheriff Connelly came around the back of one of the other saloons he came face to face with the two men and opened fire.

The men, both caught of guard by such a close encounter fired wildly, one of them missing entirely while Sheriff Connelly remained calm and fired, striking the man dead center. As the man keeled over Sheriff Connelly turned his gun to the other man but the second man managed to get off a shot of his own before he could do so, the bullet striking the sheriff in the side and causing his body to buckle to the right. Connelly tried to take aim as best he could and fired several times dropping the man where he stood. His gun hand dropped as he clutched his wounded side with his left hand, the pain radiating throughout his midsection forcing him to lean against the side of the building as he tried to fight through the pain.

He took several steps forward trying to continue on, but soon realized that he was already becoming weak from blood loss and the pain. He leaned his back against the wall and slowly slid down it to the ground in a seated position his head swaying and his thoughts growing foggy. He swung his right arm into his lap still holding his revolver there in case someone else came along and surprised him though in his current condition he doubted he would be able to put up much of a fight if they did. He tried to move once, but quickly abandoned the notion and accepted the fact that he would have to remain there until someone found him, all the while hoping it wouldn't be any more of Quincey's men.

# CHAPTER TWENTY-ONE

Frank Quincey was combing the inside of one of the saloons when he heard shooting coming from behind the building where he had just sent two of his men. One of the men had been Fox.

"Fox!" he called out, but there was no answer even though he knew he was close enough to the back door that the man should have heard him. "FOX!" he called out again, this time even louder, but still there was nothing. "Hughes!" he called out to the second man. Nothing. Although he convinced himself that they must have been shooting at someone farther down the backs of the buildings, for the first time in his adult life, Frank Quincy was worried.

Quincey walked over to the front door of the saloon with two of his men while the remaining four were dispersed throughout the other side of the street searching buildings for the stagecoach passengers. He wished that Red Bear had been there with them, but the indian had left them once they were close to Hurley unwilling to set foot in another town to settle a quarrel that had nothing to do with him.

Quincey wondered if the other group of his men that had

entered town next to the livery stables and freight office had any success, but at the same time he noticed that the shooting on that end of town had grown strangely quiet except for an occasional shot here and there.

The three men split up with Quincey cautiously walking outside and down the boardwalk while the other two men stopped and searched each store that they passed. The going was slow, but Quincey was determined to find the person he was looking for by going through as many people as was necessary in order to do that. He had no problem killing everyone that was left in town if that was what it took to make sure he had the right person and he was willing to prove it.

Deputy Wills and Cord were coming up the boardwalk towards the sheriff's office when they saw Quincey and two of his men a hundred feet away darting in and out of buildings apparently searching for them. Cord and Quincey saw each other at the same time and each opened fire as the two men with Quincey were forced to hide in the same doorway.

Cord got off a shot just as Quincey did the same with neither shot finding a target. Each man was hiding inside the doorway of a store waiting for the other one to make the first move. After several tense seconds, Quincey spoke first.

"You there! Let's talk!"

"I'm listening!" Cord responded.

"No one else has to die. I just want the one who killed my brother at the stage!"

"You found him!"

Quincey wasn't prepared to hear such a statement. He had finally found the man responsible and he was right here in front of him. He could feel the hatred brewing inside of him. "How do I know you're really the one and not just someone trying to cover for the real killer?"

"Your brother's name was Virgil, slender, mustache, brown hair, floppy black hat, rode a black and white paint."

The description sent chills down Quincey's neck. This was the man. This was what all the tracking was for. This was who he needed to kill. "Let's settle this now!" Quincey called out. "Just you and me! Everyone else stays out of it!"

"Out in the street!" Cord stated.

Cord looked back at Deputy Wills. The man had a deeply concerning look plastered on his face. "Don't do it. You can't trust him."

"I know," Cord answered back, "but this has to end before any more innocent people get hurt. This isn't this town's fight. I do this now and it'll all be over, one way or another."

"Sheriff Connelly wouldn't approve of this," Deputy Wills stated.

"Sheriff Connelly isn't here," Cord pointed out as he checked his revolver. "We don't even know if he's still alive. He could be laying out there somewhere right now hurt. No, this has to stop and it has to stop now."

"I can't let you do this, Cord, no matter how right you think you are."

"Tom, if you're going to arrest me then arrest me. Otherwise, stay here."

Deputy Wills looked Cord in the eyes and could see that he was determined to carry out his plan. He knew he should try to stop him, but he also knew it wouldn't do any good.

"Good luck," Deputy Wills advised him. Cord responded with a quick nod. He had decided that he was finally tired of running. This had to end now.

"What's it gonna be?" Quincey called out from the silence. "You already changed your mind?"

"I'm coming out!" Cord yelled as he limped from around the stoop and out onto the boardwalk. He saw Quincey step out as well, the two men locking eyes as each cautiously made their way out onto the street. Quincey's two men who were with him stayed back out of sight. The four men who had been searching stores across the street also stopped their movements, as well, in order to watch what was about to unfold.

Quincey stopped walking and stood his ground as Cord did the same. Quincey glared at the man who had killed Virgil, his thirst to kill him only getting stronger the longer he stared at him. He no longer cared if he survived just as long as he knew Cord was dead. He took in Cord's face long and hard for the first and last time.

"What's your name?" Quincey asked.

"Cord Chantry."

"Frank Quincey."

"Yeah, I know who you are."

"So, you're the one who murders young men," Quincey said accusingly, looking his disgust.

"Only ones who rob and try to kill innocent people," Cord stated flatly. "Was the money really worth all of this bloodshed?"

The comment angered Quincey even more than he already was. "I don't even care about the money, anymore. It was his idea to rob that stage. But you still shouldn't have shot him."

"Then you shouldn't have sent a boy to do a man's job."

"I didn't send him," Quincey said through gritted teeth. "But you did murder him."

"That's strong talk coming from you, of all people."

"I've been after you for a long time."

Cord stared at him with cold eyes."Well, now you found me."

Quincey went for his gun.

Frank Quincey was fast, but Cord was a little faster, firing just as Quincey's gun was leveling at him. Cord's shot hit

Quincey in the right side of his chest, knocking him back-wards and causing him to stumble a couple of feet before he lost his balance and landed on his back. Before the smoke even had a chance to clear Quincey's men began piling out onto the street from both sides, all of them firing as they ran over to assist Quincey. The storm of bullets was over-whelming as Cord ran on his injured leg towards the nearest store where Deputy Wills was still standing. Wills leaned around the corner firing into the mix to provide as much cover as he could.

Tell was unable to help defend Cord since he had gone inside the saloon to come downstairs while the shooting was taking place. Cord had almost managed to make it back to the store front when a bullet clipped his injured leg instantly dropping him to the ground. Deputy Wills stepped out from his cover and grabbed Cord's free arm and began pulling him towards the store with his left hand as he fired wildly towards the men with his gun hand. At the same time, Nathan had emerged from the sheriff's office and started laying cover for Cord and Deputy Wills to help them make their escape. By the time Deputy Wills had managed to pull Cord back behind the stoop of the store Tell emerged from the front door of the saloon just as Quincey's men had gotten him off of the street and disappeared between buildings.

Deputy Wills pulled his handkerchief from around his neck and started tying off Cord's newest wound as he leaned against the door.

"Ughh!" Cord moaned loudly, seething from the pain as Wills tightened the knot. "Leave it to me to get shot twice in the same leg!"

"This things really bleeding and you didn't help the first wound out by doing that," Wills advised him as he continued tying it off.

Cord tried to turn his head far enough to look down the

street where Quincey had been. "Where's Quincey?" he asked as he glanced down in the direction and saw no one.

"He's gone," Deputy Wills said as he finished tying off the bandage. "Tell went after them. Now, be still or I won't be able to slow the bleeding."

"He can't take all of them on by himself."

"Well, Nathan isn't in any condition to go after them and we still don't know where the sheriff is."

"Somebody come help me!" they heard Tell suddenly yell as he came from around the front corner of a building onto the boardwalk. When Cord and Deputy Wills looked in that direction, they saw Tell struggling trying to carry Sheriff Connelly in his arms. He was trying to stay on his feet as he came towards them. Wills glanced at Tell and then glanced back at Cord.

"Go! Go help him!" Cord exclaimed.

Deputy Wills jumped up and ran over to meet Tell, getting to him just as Tell's legs were starting to give and he began to feel as if he were going to drop the wounded man. Wills helped take over the majority of the man's weight from Tell with each one hanging his arms around their necks and dragging him down the boardwalk. They struggled until they made it the last short distance to the sheriff's office. Nathan, Holbrook and Madeline were standing in the door as they brought the unconscious sheriff in and laid him on the bunk in the first cell.

"I'll go get Doc Reynolds!" Wills proclaimed as he darted out the door and up the street towards the church while Madeline pulled back Sheriff Connelly's vest to check the severity of his gunshot and saw that the wound was still bleeding. "I need something, anything you can find, to hold on it to slow down the bleeding," Madeline called out.

"I'll look," Holbrook announced as he left her side and

went back into the office. A minute later he came back with one of the sheriff's clean shirts. "Will this do?"

"Yeah, thank you," Madeline answered as she took the shirt and began pressing it down onto the wound. She continued checking the wound until Deputy Wills arrived with Doc Reynolds. Madeline stood and stepped back to give him room to come in and check on the sheriff. As Doctor Reynolds went to work, Madeline walked back out to join the others.

"How is he?" Cord asked as he propped his injured leg up onto the side of the desk.

"The doctor doesn't know," she admitted. "He said it looks bad, but he's not exactly sure just how bad until he gets a better look."

"This is all my fault," Cord stated, his voice racked with guilt. "I shouldn't have brought this trouble here."

"This isn't your fault. It's Frank Quincey's fault," Tell chimed in.

"You didn't have a choice," Nathan said. "You did what you thought was best for all of us."

Madeline nodded her head in agreement. "If you had gone into Benton Springs it would have been just as bad, in fact it would probably have been even worse, because you would have been in his town, playing by his rules."

"That doesn't help the sheriff," Cord stated. "And what happened to Quincey?"

"I was going after them when I saw the sheriff laying with his back against the wall at the back of the building, bleeding and unconscious. I had to take care of him so I lost Quincey. Sorry."

"No, no, no, you did the right thing," Cord assured him.

The group sat around with very little talking while they waited for Doc Reynolds to come out with any news. The minutes turned into almost an hour before he emerged from the back room where the cell was. His face had a tired, distraught look about it.

"Well, I think I've managed to stop the bleeding, but he's a long ways from being out of danger. The next few hours are going to be crucial. You'll need to keep a close eye on him. I'm going back to my office to get a few things."

"Do we need to bring him over there?" Deputy Wills asked.

"No, he can't be moved. It'll undo everything I've done. No, he's going to have to stay put, at least until he's out of the woods, if he even makes it."

# CHAPTER TWENTY-TWO



Cord and Nathan sat in the Regal Saloon having a drink, talking quietly. Both had been recuperating since their fight with Frank Quincey two days before, each discussing their plans to move on now that they had healed enough to travel. During their talk the discussion of Quincey's whereabouts came up, but Cord conceded that no one had seen or heard from him since the gunfight nor was it known if he had even survived his injuries. They also talked briefly about Holbrook Sanders leaving town to continue his job with the railroad, of losing Billy Richmond and about River Holloway and how he had not surfaced, either.

The two men left the saloon, Nathan carrying his saddlebags and rifle and Cord using a cane as the two walked over to the waiting stage. They turned to one another as they stood on the boardwalk waiting for the driver to give the go ahead to finish loading.

"I would have thought you wouldn't be in too much of a hurry to get back on a stagecoach any time soon considering what your last ride was like," Cord said jokingly.

"Yeah, I like to tempt fate," Nathan responded with a smile. "Or maybe you just brought me bad luck."

"I'd wager it was the second one."

Nathan extended his hand as they shook. "Well, good luck in Benton Springs," he said.

"Good luck in Haynes Station."

"I guess getting my arm broken was a sign. Building railroads is hard on the body. I don't want to age before my time."

The driver came out of the stage office carrying his own saddlebags. "Stage is leaving, folks. Grab a seat," he added as he tossed his saddlebags up to the foreman and climbed up and into his seat.

"Well, if you ever need anything," Cord said, "just let me know."

"Same here."

Nathan opened the door of the stage and allowed two other men who were already waiting to step in before he climbed in behind them and closed the door. Cord stood on the boardwalk and watched as the driver untied the reins from the front brake and after disengaging it, whipped the reins with a call as the stage started rolling. Cord remained on the boardwalk until the stage was firmly on its way, trailed by a cloud of dust and quickly becoming a speck in the distance. He limped over to the sheriff's office to find Deputy Wills sitting at the desk going through wanted posters.

"Hey," Cord spoke on his way over to the nearest chair, making a sigh of relief as he sat down.

"How's the leg?"

"Still favoring it. Doc says I'll probably have a slight limp when it's all said and done."

"Still haven't gotten used to using a cane, I see," Deputy Wills said with an amused grin.

"No, I hate this thing, but it's the only way for me to get around unless you want to see me move in slow motion."

"At least you're still moving around."

The comment reminded Cord. "Speaking of which, how's the sheriff?"

"Doc Reynolds said he's going to be okay, but he still needs to take it easy, at least for the time being so it's a good thing you could hang around for awhile until he's back on his feet enough to work."

"How could I refuse? You were willing to make me a deputy."

"How does it feel to wear a badge?"

"It takes a little getting used to. And it worked out good for me. I wouldn't be much good working a ranch right now, anyway."

"So, have you seen Madeline today?"

"Yeah, I ran into her at the restaurant getting breakfast. She told me she was heading out later today on the afternoon stage."

"Well, it's not like you won't be around her," Deputy Wills pointed out. "You'll both be in Benton Springs."

Cord and Deputy Wills continued talking until it was time to make their rounds of the town. When they got back to the sheriff's office Madeline was there writing Cord a note.

"Oh, hi," she said sheepishly as she abandoned writing and crumpled up the paper and tossed it into the trash can. "I thought I'd missed you."

"I'm glad you didn't," Cord admitted with his own awkward demeanor. Deputy Wills passed him a sly grin and stepped over to the jail cells as if he had a reason to do so just to give them privacy.

"So..." Cord also tried to begin, but couldn't find the right words.

"So..." she started to say something, but paused from a lack of words.

"Look, Madeline, I owe you an apology. I never gave you a decent chance. I just assumed you were like all the other women in my life who abandoned or hurt me. I didn't give you the benefit of the doubt. I'm sorry."

There was a long, uncomfortable pause until Madeline finally become too flustered to come up with anything to say. "I understand, and you're forgiven," she added with an awkward smile. "Well, I guess I need to be going. The stage leaves in less than half an hour."

"I'll walk you over there," Cord offered, which was met with his own awkward smile. The two headed towards the door and passed Deputy Wills standing back in the cell area.

"Goodbye, Deputy," she said as she smiled to him.

"Ma'am."

As Madeline started walking through the front door Cord ducked down and retrieved the note from the trash and stuffed it into his vest pocket before she saw him. He followed her out the door as he shot Deputy Wills an elated grin of satisfaction that he was escorting her over to the stage office. When they got there they nervously sat inside at a table making small talk until the driver stuck his head inside the room and announced the departure.

"Folks, stage leaves in five minutes," he stated as he turned and began loading passengers bags atop the stage-coach. Upon hearing the news, Madeline stood and walk outside as Cord brought her bags and handed them to the driver who passed them up top before Madeline turned to face Cord one final time.

"Take care of yourself."

"You, too."

They looked at each other, he wanting to kiss her but not

knowing whether it would be met with acceptance or disdain and she not knowing how to react to their separation.

He left it with an awkward pause as she gave him an uncomfortable smile before he grabbed her hand and helped her up into the stagecoach. She sat next to the nearest window and looked out at him with a silent smile as the rest of the passengers boarded and took their seats. As the door was closed, the finality of it took hold.

"Maybe I'll see you around Benton Springs," he suggested.

"Hopefully," she responded as he floundered nervously.

As Cord watched the driver call the stage into motion for the second time that day and watched her being driven away he remembered the note and pulled it from his pocket:

*Cord,*

*Considering the circumstances, I wish we had gotten more of a chance to get to know each other. Maybe when you make it to Benton Springs we can have a cup of coffee together. Look me up.*

*~ Madeline*

He looked up at the stage disappearing across the landscape, his hope renewed as a smile covered his face.

www.ingramcontent.com/pod-product-compliance
Lightning Source LLC
Chambersburg PA
CBHW021149190726
48288CB00008B/2895